NOONDAY DARK

Noonday Dark

CHARLES DEMERS

 Douglas & McIntyre

Douglas and McIntyre (2013) Ltd.
P.O. Box 219, Madeira Park, BC, VON 2H0
www.douglas-mcintyre.com

Edited by Caroline Skelton
Cover design by Anna Comfort O'Keeffe
Typesetting by Libris Simas Ferraz / Onça Publishing
Printed and bound in Canada
Printed on 100% recycled paper

Douglas and McIntyre acknowledges the support of the Canada Council
for the Arts, the Government of Canada, and the Province of British
Columbia through the BC Arts Council.

Library and Archives Canada Cataloguing in Publication

Title: Noonday dark / Charles Demers.
Names: Demers, Charles, 1980- author.
Description: Series statement: A Dr. Annick Boudreau Mystery ; 2
Identifiers: Canadiana (print) 20220180695 | Canadiana (ebook)
    20220180709 | ISBN 9781771623285(softcover) | ISBN 9781771623292
    (EPUB)
Classification: LCC PS8607.E533 N66 2022 | DDC C813/.6—dc23

For my brother, Nick

I try hard to remember the phrase but I can't speak the
language
just here for a couple of days
me puedes ayudar
[. . .]
I follow you into the maze and I'm struck with the anguish
just here for a couple of days
me puedes ayudar

Waiting for the wave to take me down
I could never stay in one place for too long
Trying to be brave
But it wears me out
Carries me away, far away
Well, I'm gone

— ASHLEIGH BALL,
"Me Puedes Ayudar" [Can You Help Me?]

1

"I HEARD THAT Guns N' Roses made it official. It's now *except* for cold November rain." She smiled with the bottom half of her face, while the top half was already disavowing the joke, rolling her eyebrows over and away with a knowing charm. Not too long ago, they would have said that Danielle was too beautiful to be a comedian, but the world, except for a few stragglers, knew better than that now. They might also have said, back then, that she was too beautiful to be depressed, to have anything to be depressed about, but they were starting to catch on that that wasn't how that worked, either. Danielle pushed a curtain of dark blonde hair behind her ear as she let the last of the smile simmer off from her lips, looking out at the grey Vancouver downpour that was hitting the window with the intensity of make-believe rain in movies.

"Day sixteen," said Dr. Annick Boudreau by way of commiseration. "Right through the kids' Hallowe'en and the grown-ups' election. My mother keeps calling from Halifax, asking if the weather app on her phone is broken."

Danielle smiled.

"Speaking of which," Dr. Boudreau continued, "I don't think I've seen you since the election. That must have been pretty satisfying, your guy winning. By a pretty good margin, too."

"Yeah. My guy." Danielle smiled dismissively, then shrugged. "It was nice. There was a party at the Sylvia Hotel. The campaign rented out the whole bar and restaurant downstairs. It's so beautiful down there. You know how I am with a crowd, at least without a stage to keep me safe. I couldn't take it for too long. The campaign booked some rooms upstairs, too, so I just went, spent the night. Woke up looking out over English Bay."

"Very nice. Rain or no rain."

"It was amazing. But I managed to stay downstairs through to the end of Berto's victory speech." She smiled again.

"Yeah? Did he use any of your jokes?"

"He did, yeah. A couple." Danielle tried to keep the glow of pride from her face when she answered, but her thrill was apparent in the rush of colour to her cheeks and the shy contentment at the corners of her mouth. "It was so nice to hear them in, like, a crowd—that was a first. Usually, in the campaign, I didn't get to be there for that—to hear them land. Of course the only people who know I wrote them are me, Berto, a couple people from the campaign, and you."

"One day the truth will come out, I'm sure."

Danielle laughed softly. "Right, maybe."

"Will you keep working for Rossi now that he's mayor?"

"No." She shook her head, and though the smile was still on her face some of the shine came out of it. "No, now that the daily speeches are over, they don't need jokes. They might come to me for a bit of punch-up here and there, for

2

ribbon-cutting-type things. But I'm back to just stand-up now. Freelancing."

"You seem okay about that."

"Definitely. No, I'm—I'm feeling really good, Dr. Boudreau. Things are going really well for once. Things with the guy, the guy from the campaign?"

"Yeah?"

"They're really nice."

"That's wonderful."

"I mean, November kind of always sucks. The rain. I mean it sucks because it's November, but it's also—I often think about my dad this time of year. I think about calling him, and then I imagine how it would go, and I just . . ." she trailed off. Danielle turned to look out the window, as if confirming that the city's grey, sodden November was still outside, waiting for her.

"Why this time of year in particular, do you think? Is it his birthday around now, or . . ."

Danielle shook her head. "No. This feels weird to say because he was never a soldier or anything but I think it's because of Remembrance Day. That's so stupid, right? For some reason, I just so associate it with his . . . *change*. With, like, what he's become."

"Why do you think that is?"

Danielle shrugged her shoulders inside of her large, cream-coloured cable-knit sweater, even though she knew the answer. "When I was eight years old, one of the first times he ever spoke to me about politics as an equal—like, not drilling something into me to memorize but actually reasoning it out with me? It was after I'd told him I'd been

chosen to recite 'In Flanders Fields' at the school assembly."
She quickly flashed another bashful-pride smile, then let
the elegant features of her long face settle into something
more tender. "He sat with me and we read the poem and we
talked about the words and what they meant, what his problems with it were. We really talked about it, how fucked up
it was to ask little kids to 'take up our quarrel with the foe,'
and how World War One and World War Two were related,
but they were different, and how this necessary war against
Hitler had been used to shine up this senseless bloodbath
from decades earlier, and I mean—like I'm eight, right? I
know I was only a kid but it feels like my first adult memory
of my dad, if that makes sense?"

"That completely makes sense," Dr. Boudreau said.
She was a cognitive behavioural therapist, not a talk therapist—she had no couch, no framed cartoons from the *New
Yorker*—but she had learned in her years at the office that
there were times to let her patients speak at length; to let
them tell a bit of the stories that they had pieced together
about themselves.

"I knew my dad was a writer before that. But I never
really knew what words meant to him, ideas. Or like, not in
that concrete of a way. You know?"

"Absolutely," said Annick, fingering the side of the cold
mug on her desk and thinking of her own parents across the
country with a pang of longing; thinking, in spite of herself and as she did so often lately, what sort of thing it was
to be someone's daughter, and what it might be like to be
somebody's mom.

"And now, this new version of him. I read his blog yesterday. I don't know why I do it—I mean, I guess it's my only contact with him, but it always just leaves me feeling so sad. And anyway he's just, he's writing about the betrayal of Canada's warrior history and appeasement in the face of China and Iran, maybe gender studies departments, and it's like I can't even recognize him. Like, other people's dads are supposed to be this way, I understand that. But mine? God no." Instead of crying, she laughed again. "But aside from that? I feel great. I mean, I feel *me* great. I'll never be like one of those bitches in the yogurt commercials, smile so hard they release a blood clot. But all in all? I'm not crying, I'm getting to sleep around one-thirty, waking up around nine-thirty, ten, I'm getting outside. When I think back to how things were last summer, before the campaign? I don't want to exaggerate, but the difference is like night and day."

Annick smiled, nodding slowly, not in the way she'd nod to give assent or to confirm an order but in the way one nods to music, just before dancing. Sometimes it was hard for patients to tell from inside just how much things had changed, how far they had come. But Danielle, whom she had been seeing for eighteen months, and who for most of that time could be reliably counted on to break down in heaving sobs at one or multiple points in any given session, had worked hard with her, and had begun righting her sails. For all her years in the doctor's chair, Annick wasn't yet past the point of being proud of her patients in moments like these, or proud of herself. She doubted she ever would get past it. She certainly never wanted to.

"I can't tell you how great it is to hear this, Danielle. And since I know you, and that you're the Queen of Understatement, and that there's no credit you won't instantly brush off," Danielle smiled and batted away the accusation ironically, "I'm going to tell you the one thing people coming out of a major depression forget to do."

"What?"

"Remember how far they've come. You done good," Dr. Boudreau said, reaching absently for the mug of milky coffee in order to brace herself against the sight of the November chill outside. Smiling at her patient, Dr. Boudreau took a long sip of the coffee before spraying it back into the mug with a gag.

"I'm so sorry," she said, her white cheeks going nearly mauve with embarrassment.

"Are you okay?" asked Danielle, with her wide eyes playing the role of sincerity this time, her mouth betraying them with a smirk.

"Yeah, sorry. That was yesterday's coffee. This one," she said, hefting an identical mug from the clinic's collection, "is the one I was after. Sorry."

"You don't have to keep apologizing."

"No, I know. I just—that wasn't what I was expecting."

2

WHEN ANNICK ARRIVED, the calamari was already on the table. Her boyfriend, Philip, sat looking up from the plate with an almost unreadable mixture of guilt, pleasure and accomplishment written across his face.

"I'm impressed. The fact that you were able to wait for me to get here before starting is almost enough to make up for you not standing for a gentlelady arriving to table."

"All those chivalrous rules are from the days before watches and cell phones. Those women didn't know how late they were."

Philip leaned forward for a kiss, and Annick bit his earlobe.

"Seriously, love, you could have started." Once again, he gave her the look: guilt, pleasure, pride, all in roughly equal measure. She smiled out of one side of her mouth. "What? What is this look?"

"This is the second plate."

Annick let loose an explosive burst of laughter that briefly set the almost invisible waiter who had begun filling her glass with sparkling mineral water off his gait, splashing the tablecloth.

"I'm so sorry!" she said.

"Please," said the waiter, flattening his fingers in a deci-
sive bid to end the conversation, making it clear that the
only insult that he could not bear was the idea that the service was not entirely within his control. "Tonight's specials
are a steelhead trout served with mushroom risotto, and rabbit with asparagus and fingerling potatoes. I'll let you have
a moment with the menu. Would madame like something
from the bar?"

Annick turned to Philip. "Gimme a hit of what you got?"
He nodded and passed her a wineglass the diameter of
a salad dish, the bottom eighth of which was filled with a
wine so red it was purple. Annick stuck her nose in the glass,
sniffed, took a small sip and made the sound of *le petit mort.*
"Oh, that tastes like an old leather wingback chair."

"She means that as a compliment," said Philip apologetically. The waiter bowed his head.

"A nine-ounce glass, please. Thank you," said Annick.
She turned back to Philip and the calamari. "Somehow
you're still going to feel entitled to half this plate though,
aren't you?"

"I mean really, when you think about it, since it was my
idea to order it . . ."

Annick looked at Philip, first within the context of his
being hers, then within the context of the restaurant, then
within the context of the neighbourhood; she smiled.

"You happy?" she asked.

Philip nodded, scooping a ring of the best, most buttery-
smooth calamari in the city into his mouth.

Both Annick and Philip had grown up socioeconom-
ically south and geographically east of the Coal Harbour

condominium that now afforded their childless, upper middle-class professional lives such breathtaking views of the water, the mountains and Stanley Park. But where Annick's "east" took her all the way across the country, to the Acadian shores of the Atlantic, Philip was a son of East Vancouver, the once-tough semi-suburban half of the city that now rested its old habits and attitudes uneasily on lots each worth more than a million dollars. Philip had grown up during the architectural reign of the Vancouver Special, considered, at the time of his youth, to be the tacky embarrassment of every V5 postal code; pure testament to blue-collar immigrant utility over form. The two-storey square-footage maximizers were primarily inhabited by either Italian families or, like Philip's, Chinese, though every once in a while a Portuguese or Vietnamese property holder might surprise you. Over the years, as both the neighbourhood and Philip had made their climbs up the class hierarchy, the reputation of the Vancouver Special had climbed with them, and now that their architectural advance had ceased and even retreated, the city had adopted the unique little houses as a sort of architectural mascot, like a bulldog so ugly that it was cute.

But given how quickly and how enormously things had changed, Philip cherished the little bits of East Vancouver that looked and felt exactly as he had left them: East Side Billiards, the pool hall on Nanaimo and Hastings, which still featured hand-drawn and photocopied warnings against ripping the table felts; the PNE fairgrounds, which somehow retained all of their carney seediness summer after summer; and the Centre for Italian Culture, with its language-class advertisements, its adjacent elder care homes, and its inevitably fantastic restaurant, Piazza D'Angelo. The Lee family had come here once a year, every year, to celebrate Philip's mother's birthday, and he had described it to Annick as "East Van fancy," before she told him that that description now suited him pretty perfectly, too.

"That rabbit sounds good, huh?"

"It does," answered Philip, after swallowing the last bite of his half of the second plate of calamari. He dipped a piece of bread in olive oil. "But I'm not coming to D'Angelo and not getting pasta."

The restaurant was full tonight, pretty good for a rainy evening in November, except for a long empty table in the middle of the dining area, though it was marked "Reserved." As she scanned the room, Annick felt a bump at her side and looked down to see a two-year-old girl with short, thick, Mediterranean curls and precociously pierced ears, grinning widely and wildly. Her chin and cheeks were shining slick with teething slobber, in stark contrast with the just-so baby doll dress and bracelets in which she was clearly done up for something special.

"*Allô, chouette*," said Annick. "Hi! Aren't you a big girl? *Oui!*"

"Be go!" confirmed the toddler in triumph, just as her father ran up behind her and scooped her up into his arms.

"Giuseppina, where'd you go? Where'd you go, Geppa?"

"Be go!"

"Sorry about that, guys. Somebody got away from Nonno and Nonna's anniversary table."

"Oh, please," said Annick. "Anybody ever makes you apologize for this little treasure, you kick them right in the nuts for me."

The young father, who had already started into his pro forma smile, took a half second to register his confusion at Annick's response. As he pivoted away, Giuseppina continued to deliver the open-and-shut goodbye that babies master before learning to wave their hands. Annick turned back to Philip.

"I guess I shouldn't have said 'nuts' in front of the baby, right?"

"Probably not. Some kids are allergic."

"Asshole," she said, whipping him under the table with her thick linen napkin. Through dinner, and dessert, and a cappuccino that she savoured as much as any of it—the only coffee Annick ever sweetened with sugar was an after-dinner coffee—she found herself checking in on baby Giuseppina regularly, watching her pulling at her mother's hair; laughing at the faces that the adults around the table competed to make for her; falling asleep on her grandmother's shoulder.

"You ready to go?"

"What?"

"Listen, I feel bad for not standing when you came in. Let me assist you with your coat."

Annick stood, and as she slipped her hand into the sleeve, leaning back to let Philip kiss her softly on the ear, a commotion began by the entrance of the restaurant. A series of competitively demonstrative Italian greetings had begun, with audible well-wishing and backslapping, and both Annick and Philip craned to see what was going on.

"Wow," said Philip. "It's the new mayor."

The newly elected mayor, Alberto Rossi, was another product of the Vancouver Special era of East Vancouver—though he had grown up in one of the Italian ones. Now a handsome package of olive and silver, he had ten years on Philip, but had graduated from the same high school. His story, having been rehearsed so many times recently, was well known by now throughout the city: an East Van kid from when the streets were still fairly mean, he'd been a teenaged lifeguard at Britannia Pool on Commercial Drive, which had led him into the city workers' unions. Throughout his twenties he'd been one of the province's youngest, and certainly handsomest, labour leaders, before running for city council at twenty-nine. A practicing and progressive-leaning Roman Catholic with a soft spot for Francis of Assisi and a glancing familiarity with the bigger names in liberation theology; married to his high-school girlfriend, also an avid cyclist and green campaigner: Rossi was hard to slot into culture war pigeonholes, and so he largely avoided them.

Less than two weeks after his landslide triumph over the faceless WASP candidate run by the undead civic right-wing party—stuck deep in the city's West Side and distant past—Rossi had already had his first scandal, walking back a major campaign promise to phase out the trucking corridor along Clark Drive, which turned into Knight Street, and had for as long as anyone could remember been the north–south truck route from the port to the suburbs and back. But tonight, none of the many people who were angry at him

were in attendance. He was, instead, the city's triumph-
ant first Italian-Canadian mayor, at the Centre for Italian
Culture's restaurant, and the big empty table in the middle
of it all was reserved for him and his entourage.

Rossi shepherded his party to their table, along with the
typically low-key maître d' who was, at present, bordering
on unctuous. Rossi's parents seemed to be there, along with
his wife, Luciana, the labour lawyer turned consultant for
multiple levels of centre-left government—regally beautiful
and full-bodied, the thick mane of her argent-brown hair
cropped into a shining bob. His young campaign manager,
Tavleen Dosanjh, who had transitioned seamlessly into the
leadership team at City Hall, was there, though not looking
up from her phone; also present was Kingsley Davis, a red-
hot political consultant whose willingness to step down from
the heights of federal and provincial politics to the smaller
arena of the municipal had been a major story for one of
the election's many news cycles and taken as a sure sign of
Rossi's seriousness; there was Olivia Preston, Rossi's tall
and elegant slate-mate and just-appointed deputy mayor;
there were also sundry middle-aged men and women whom
Annick did not recognize. And there, standing quietly at the
back of the group, still dressed in the sweater she had been
wearing to their session, a bit of makeup her only visible con-
cession to the formality of the occasion, was Danielle. Here,
though, there was nothing of the onstage charismatic or offstage wisecracker in the way she carried herself. Danielle's
smiles and greetings were polite but looked wooden; she
took part in the big round of greetings, but withdrew whenever someone else pulled attention and she had the chance.

She warmed slightly as she was approached by a tall man with grey-blond hair, average-looking but in incredible shape, who leaned in to whisper something conspiratorially in her ear.

"You recognize the other guy too, right? The white guy. Where do I know him from?" asked Philip innocently, making Annick realize that her wine had slowed her down. She should never have been staring at her patient that way; even an indiscretion that small could compromise her confidentiality.

Annick shrugged. "Yeah, I don't know where he's from," she answered, telling no lies.

Like a cruise director, Rossi guided everyone to their seats as though Piazza D'Angelo was his own dining room; the gravity in the room turned and churned with his every micro-gesture, every wave of his long, brown fingers. And when he came to Danielle he put his hand on her back, said something to her that looked like he was making a joke, and Danielle made the generous face that very funny people make when people who aren't very funny try to make them laugh.

Despite Annick's wine-slowed look, Danielle hadn't noticed her yet, so Annick took Philip by the arm, kissed his cheek, and motioned with her head towards the door.

"Enough of this working-class authenticity. Take me back to my soulless yuppie palace."

"Sure, let me just grab a calamari to go."

Annick smiled and pinched Philip's somehow-flat stomach, taking one last look at sleeping baby Giuseppina on her way out the door, and saw Danielle listening graciously as

Mrs. Rossi told the table a story. Philip opened the door onto the late-evening darkness, and the punishing hiss of the rain broke Annick's idyll.

"You know what's weird, that you'd never expect?" said Philip as he let Annick out the door before him. "Rossi's actually really funny."

"Hm," she said.

3

"YOU DEAL WITH DEPRESSION in a professional capacity, don't you?"

"I do indeed."

"So tell me this party isn't a flagrant workplace hazard, then."

Annick laughed as Bonnie Ashford, local crime reporter for the CBC, threw the dregs of a tumbler of Scotch down her long, aristocratic throat before continuing into her criticism of the public broadcaster. "A Christmas party, only it's a Winter Holiday Party, only it's in the middle of fucking November because the suits don't want to pay what it costs to rent a place like this out in December."

"Well, why pay for December real estate if it's not technically a Christmas party?"

"Hey, whose side are you on, anyway? At least the sushi's good. Last year, on my good name, they tried to feed us Costco sausage rolls. When I started in this business the parties were a lot more lechy but a lot better catered."

"You know, all in all I think I'd still take that deal," Annick said.

"I suppose you're right. Keep your sweaty hands out of the small of my back, and I'll buy my own canapés. Sweetie, your head doesn't get cold like that, so short? Even in the winter?"

"Bonnie, you were just complaining it wasn't winter yet."

"Christmas, darling—it's not *Christmas* yet. You haven't been in Vancouver long enough. You Maritimers with your four seasons, your precious colour-changing leaves. Here 'winter' just means wet and dark. It's winter as soon as it isn't summer."

Annick smiled and pulled absently at the pixie bangs of her in-between haircut, then lifted and pulled from the rum and Kahlúa she'd had to pay for herself when the bartender told her that her drink ticket only covered house wine or domestic beer. She didn't often miss her shaved head, though she had to admit it had been far more satisfying to play with than the spiky strands she had been able to grow back so far. She was happy to have finally been found by Bonnie, one of the only people from Philip's work whom she really knew or cared for, even—perhaps especially—when the reporter, who knew a thing or two about sailing, was a few sheets to the wind. On their way to the party, walking up from Coal Harbour into downtown under a shared umbrella—their heads dry, their feet cold and damp—Philip had been full of the usual promises to stay close to her side, to keep their party appearance to a merciful minimum. Now, on the other side of the crowded room from Annick, he was proving to a gaggle of howling sports reporters that he could indeed do The Worm.

All of this was, of course, to be expected, and as a keen observer of patterns in human psychology Annick hadn't prepared herself for either a short evening or one in which she was well attended to by her once-a-year breakdancing boyfriend. But the prospect of some time in the personal pull of the magnetic event that was Bonnie Ashford could make up for most of that. Bonnie dressed like a woman who might occasionally lend Diane Keaton some of her less sophisticated items, and for the life of her Annick couldn't tell what it was about this particular white shirt and black jacket—but was it white? or ivory? was it a jacket or a blazer?—that made it so qualitatively unlike any white shirt and black jacket that she would ever own, but she had long given up any bewildered resentment and learned simply to enjoy the Old Money puzzle.

"It's so good to see you, Bonnie. How have you been?"

"I've been very well, as it happens. Been a slog of a year work-wise, but I've had a bit of good news on the home front to make up for it. It was a hot summer, with all the gang stuff in the 'burbs."

"The shootings, you mean? It was wild."

Bonnie nodded. "Happens about every ten years but this cycle was a few years early. The feds extradited a big bad godfather who turned out to be the only thing holding his sons and his nephews within the bounds of good sense and military diplomacy. Then as soon as that cooled down, I rolled right into the civic election."

"Different kind of turf war."

"Sometimes. Sometimes not so much. Take our new mayor's U-turn on the truck route."

"Yeah, that was so weird. He made such a big deal about it during the election: the air pollution, the traffic, whatever.

It was central to his whole pitch and then he walked it back just, I don't know, immediately. "

"The city's done all kinds of studies—the numbers are through the roof, but nobody's ever acted on it, so along comes Rossi, the East Van avenger. Particulate matter in the air, the kids who live along Clark and Knight Street breathing it in all hours of the day—multiple elementary and high schools, community centres. That's to say nothing of the noise, tying up a huge north–south artery. The port in Tsawwassen's a going concern, on land covered by a freshly inked treaty, so it makes sense to shift at least some of the action out there. Plus, the new mayor makes a bunch of grateful East Vancouver millionaires overnight out of everyone who owns anything even close to Clark or Knight. He'd have a firewall of permanent Rossi voters to save him from any revanchism from the West Side sons of silver I grew up with."

"But then what's the catch? If it was that much of a slam dunk, wouldn't someone have done it by now? Or at the very least Rossi wouldn't have walked away like he did?"

Bonnie smiled to herself, and picked a razor-thin slice of pale yellow pickled ginger from one of the nearly empty sushi plates on the table beside the two women.

"Well," she said, raising her features archly, "let's just say that when it comes to standing up to bikers, not everyone's balls are as big as mine."

"What?" Annick nearly shouted, laughing as she swatted the sleeve of Bonnie's jacket-blazer. "What do you mean?"

"Oh, listen to me—I'm drunk."

"What do bikers have to do with anything?"

"Please, honey. The Satan's Hammer Motorcycle Club has been running the hiring hall at the Vancouver port since before my ancestors showed up with pestilence and High Church Anglicanism. You could be wet enough behind the ears to get a slap from the doctor and still wouldn't expect to see anything like one hundred percent of a shipment come in through there."

"Wow. I mean, I guess I kinda knew that—I don't know, in the way that you 'know' things about a place."

"Sure."

"Like common sense. Like back in Montréal, when I was at school, and the old-timers would tell you not to trust any business on the second floor."

"'What are they hiding up there?'"

"Exactly. But—so you think they, what, threatened Rossi? I mean it's not the Wild West."

"Annick, my love, how many kilometres did you travel from Halifax?"

"Just under six thousand."

"And in which direction, pray tell, were you moving?"

Annick smiled and swatted again, eliciting a small, subtle patrician grin from Bonnie as she leaned in for more ginger.

"But I thought Rossi was a tough guy," said Annick.

"Oh, everybody from East Van *used* to be a tough guy," Bonnie answered, dismissing the very idea with a wave of her hand.

Annick took a sip from her drink, and watched Philip over the rim of her glass on the other side of the room, popping and locking to the great amusement of people he might just as easily dismiss, on other days, as *douchebags* or *bourgie Kitsilano boys*. On a night like tonight, when he'd had a few drinks, Philip might even let slip to those softer kinds of men some stories from the years before he became a science journalist; the years that had tattooed his arms with the same types of dragons that any listless middle-class kid could shell out for now, but tattooed his brain with the kinds of memories that remained much harder to come by. The stories from in his cups weren't the ones with dark edges though—the ones with the nauseous, grinding excess of young men's violence. Tonight, at the party, they would be safely edited ex-gangster stories, comfortably in the rearview mirror.

"He went to the same school as Philip, you know? Rossi did."

"Really?"

"Yeah. We saw him the other day, at Piazza D'Angelo. Came in like King Shit." Annick reached down for a slab of pearly pink tuna sashimi, trying to gauge how long it had been sitting out at room temperature, before remembering: "Wait, what was your good news? On the home front?"

"Oh, my son! He got into art school—in your old back-yard, actually, at NSCAD."

"Oh, that's amazing!"

"Yeah," Bonnie said, licking the ginger brine from the end of her fingers with a goofy, loving face Annick had never seen her make before. "We worried about him for so long—drugs, I mean it was pot mostly for years, then mushrooms, but then things started to get a little bit more serious. The shrink said he might have been worried about me, about my work—" Bonnie seemed to realize, then, the tone with which she had said "shrink," and froze in well-mannered horror until Annick rolled her eyes in mock-offended absolution. "But he's really pulled it together."

"That's wonderful, Bonnie. I didn't—I feel bad, I didn't even know you had a son."

"Only good thing to come from husband number two. Think you guys will have kids?"

Annick shrugged nonchalantly, before worrying that her nonchalance might seem too theatrical and so she amended it by waving her hand, then drinking the last of her rum and Kahlúa.

"I never really thought about it much," she said, finally.

4

THE SMELL OF TIBETAN incense crept out from underneath her colleague's door, and Annick smiled on the way to the break room; he had his rituals, and she had hers. She pulled the carafe out of the coffee machine and felt the side of it, wincing slightly at a sharp heat she was nevertheless quite happy to discover. She filled the massive, handmade clay mug that her parents had mailed her from Bucerías, the small Canadian semi-colony in the Mexican state of Nayarit, where they had travelled to celebrate the full remission of her father's cancer. They had taken their granddaughter, Marie-Élaine—whose own chemotherapy had inspired Annick's haircut by act of impulsive solidarity, though the little girl's hair had grown back now in inverse proportion to her own fully remitted cancer—along for the sunny victory lap.

"T'ey took the cancer out of my guts, so we're gonna go get some on my skin," Annick's father would say mischievously to anyone who would listen, and some who wouldn't, and her mother would feign fresh outrage every time.

Annick liked to pour too much coffee, so that she had to drink part of it black right away if she wanted milk. She leaned back against the counter and closed her eyes, the heat at her mouth and throat, soon in her chest and belly, temporarily offsetting the slightly wet chill that hung around her feet—the heels, soles and toes—in Vancouver from just before Hallowe'en until about Shrove Tuesday. The truly punishing Maritime winters that Annick had seen had primarily been on visits to the family in New Brunswick, where the winds off the Bay of Fundy delivered sandpaper slaps to any part of an uncovered face, but there'd been plenty enough ice and snow in Halifax, not to mention during her school years in Montréal. Her arrival in Vancouver had been supposed to signal her retirement from Canadian winter.

And it had, mostly—but there was something bitterly tenacious about the tiny Vancouver winter, its sheer commitment to the bit, its relentless grey wetness, that the folks back east had been too quick to dismiss because of the flaky, Diet California city's relatively high mercury levels, in both its sashimi and its thermometers. The eastern winters were like a dramatic siege outside the castle, but the West Coast equivalent was like ten thousand peas underneath the royal mattress.

There was, first, her discovery that the difference between Dry Cold and Wet Cold wasn't merely a figment of Vancouver's lightweight imagination; it wasn't the kind of subtlety one would notice in the difference between, say, −30 or −25 off the banks of the Red River, but Annick did notice that a night in Vancouver at two or three degrees above freezing felt decidedly less comfortable than five or six degrees below any time she'd been to the prairies.

But mostly, the misery of the city's winter was its erasure of sky; the wet, grey, boxing in; the pitch darkness at four p.m.—and what it did to nearly everyone in town.

Everywhere else she'd ever lived, late fall and winter were points on the calendar when people happily bundled up in order to *get* somewhere; poured inside where it was warm, dry and handsomely lit, and spent time in each other's company. In Vancouver, almost as soon as the manic extroversion of summertime was finished, the whole city turned inward, racing to get home and put their socks on the electric baseboard heaters, throw their umbrellas in the bathtub, and inhale the humidity from saturated jackets made from unnatural materials slowly warming up inside under artificial lights that could never quite hold their own against the weight of the darkness outdoors.

A third of the way into her mug of coffee, Annick opened the fridge for milk, only to find that someone had finished the carton and left it unreplaced.

"Dammit," Annick said to herself, cursing her tea-drinking colleagues and whichever cup of bergamot travesty the last of the milk had been wasted on trying to make palatable. She grabbed the carafe again, replaced the third of black coffee she'd already drunk, and headed back to her office, this time noticing that the door to her colleague's office was open. Cedric, remarkably flexible for a man of his vintage, was bending his tall, lean frame down to pick up the meditation cushion he'd just been sitting on. Down the hall, the phone in Dr. Boudreau's office rang, and though she remembered that Marcel at reception was currently on break, Annick felt disinclined to pass up the opportunity to needle her Zen associate just for the sake of answering a phone call.

"Do we need to have the religion-in-the-workplace sensitivity clinic again?" she asked, leaning against the frame of Cedric's doorway as he replaced the cushion in a large, ornate basket of stained, braided wood.

"I wish someone had told me all those years ago," Cedric said slowly, "that I was teaming up with a woman who had all the spiritual perspicacity of Richard Dawkins reading a copy of *Charlie Hebdo*."

"That's anti-French."

"And this weather is anti-Jamaican. Tell me this isn't a subtle attempt to force me into repatriation?"

"I don't know where you get 'subtle' from."

"Sheer foolishness to build a city here in the first place."

"Well, there've been people here for at least ten thousand years. Gotta be something to recommend it."

"Two weeks of cherry blossoms. The whole city is dining out the other fifty weeks a year on those two weeks of Japanese cherry blossoms."

"I wasn't counting syllables—was that a haiku?"

"How is your day going?"

Annick shrugged, almost spilling her refilled coffee. "I'm okay. I had a no-show this morning, who was a bit of a surprise, but it actually gave me a bit of emailing room."

"And dollars to donuts, your bleeding do-gooder heart won't even charge them for the missed session," Cedric said from behind a crooked half-smile. The phone in her office began to ring again, and Annick decided to take the opportunity to escape from Cedric's professional advice-giving.

"And dollars to dharma," she said over her shoulder, "it's none of your business!"

Annick set her mug down on the desk at the third ring, and picked up in the middle of the fourth.

"Hello, Dr. Annick Boudreau, West Coast Cognitive Behavioural Therapy Clinic."

"Hello, Dr. Boudreau, this is Constable Arminder Mann from the Vancouver Police Department. Is this an okay time for you to talk?"

"I —" Annick was thrown by the woman's terse politeness, which landed with the full weight of her authority. Annick hadn't been sure, exactly, where she stood with regards to the VPD—whether she was on their Enemies List, or whether anyone there even knew her name—since her intervention on behalf of a wrongfully arrested patient. She had sent along a nose-tweaking, screw-you message to the ranking officer on the case through her patient's lawyer once she'd known that he was in the clear, but she had no idea if the lawyer had passed it along, and had often wondered, since sending it, if it had been the right call—well, hadn't so much *wondered* as known it was childish and wished that she had exercised more impulse control. Now, whenever she saw a VPD cruiser in her rearview mirror, her speed would drop to ten kilometres below the speed limit, even though Philip insisted that cops hated that even more than minor speeding. "Wh-what's this about, sorry?"

"Do you treat a patient named Danielle MacFadden?"

Annick's neck and cheeks caught fire, and the black coffee filling her stomach turned over on itself. It had been Danielle who hadn't shown up for her appointment that morning.

"I'm sorry," Annick said calmly, regaining some of her footing, as she always did when it came to the sturdier ground of defending her patients, "Whether I do or don't,

I'm not actually able to discuss that over the phone or with anyone because of privacy issues."

"Dr. Boudreau, we believe that Ms. MacFadden may have committed suicide."

Annick nearly dropped the phone from her ear as her left hand began shaking, and she caught the receiver with her right. As her heartbeat picked up she could feel her ears throbbing against the plastic of the phone, which suddenly felt clammy and off balance, and she tried to calm herself, first with two or three of the deep breaths in through the nose that Cedric had taught her, then with a large, scalding gulp of black coffee.

"We investigated Ms. MacFadden's apartment after she was reported missing and found several empty bottles of an antidepressant prescription, prescribed by her family doctor, doctor . . ." she paused, clearly searching her notes. "Dr. Tsong. When we called Dr. Tsong's office he mentioned that you were also treating Ms. MacFadden for depression. Is that correct?"

Annick fought to snap her swimming head into focus, to go over her responsibilities to Danielle in the context. As she did, she began to calm down naturally. She remembered Danielle's smile at her last session, the good news about her life and her relationship. Her growing excitement about her comedy and her prospects. There'd been the small, dull edge of the November blues, the thoughts about her father, but Danielle had been, on the whole, in a much better space.

"What I can tell you," she said, after a few seconds, "is that in my opinion, I believe that Danielle would have been at very low risk of self-harm at this time."

"Well, there was a suicide note," said Constable Mann.

5

AT THIS TIME of year, the waters of Coal Harbour were a haunted grey-green, as inscrutable and unwelcoming as the North Atlantic choppiness she'd learned in her youth. The mountains, like French royalty, were headless in the fog, and the typically expansive view from the condominium over Stanley Park and the Burrard Inlet was shrunken by the overpowering wet grey. Still, Annick had been standing at the floor-to-ceiling window for what must have been two hours, numbly not seeing what was in front of her until the lamppost lights on the seawall began to light up, and she wondered again why Philip hadn't returned her texts asking where he was.

Dr. Philomena Conte, Annick's mentor, had taken months to answer honestly when Annick had asked her what would happen, what it would be like, if and when a patient ever took their own life. A split-second's storm had passed over Dr. Conte's large and dignified features before she'd assumed an unnatural and unnerving calm, unspooling a length of comfortably clinical and well-removed bromides, expounding upon the subject with official and unsentimental guidance. Annick didn't even know what she was talking about when, months later, at the end of a large meal, in a quiet corner of a busy restaurant, her teacher, staring into the middle distance, had picked up the thread of the conversation as though just coming out of a deep sleep.

"My Aunt Lourdes, I remember her face after my cousin Carlo died, still a baby. I don't know how she felt, but that face—it was the only thing that ever looked anything like what I was feeling after that kid hanged himself."

Annick shivered and rubbed her arms, and wondered if it was possible that she could have read the situation with Danielle as wrongly as it seemed. When Annick had first started seeing her as a patient, Danielle had been at a very low point. She had been nearly as bad as any depression patient Annick had ever treated. With depression, some gained weight and some lost it, but Danielle would do both, alternately: come in for weeks with a gradually hollowing face, darkening eyes—then, in the space of a few months, fit poorly into clothes she was suddenly too big for. At night she couldn't sleep, and during the days she couldn't wake—the schedule of a working stand-up comedian only exacerbating irregular nocturnal patterns, filling her late nights with adrenaline dumps and alcohol in lieu of payment. In one session, she would rage about the mediocrities who were outstripping her in their career achievements, how she was being ignored despite her talent; the next, she would sob and bemoan what she would now identify as her own mediocrity, the fact that she couldn't excel at the only thing she'd ever really cared about. One week, she thought the world saw nothing but her looks; the next, that she'd lost or outgrown even them.

They had processed some of the trauma of her mother's sudden death from a stroke when Danielle had been just fourteen. At a time when most girls would have been pulling away from their parents to begin defining their own identities, Danielle had become, in the wake of her mother's death, inseparable from her father, Ivor MacFadden, the gruff, well-respected gadfly, local muckraker and left-wing columnist for the independent arts and news weekly, *The Lions' Gate*. She and Dr. Boudreau had worked through what had felt like a second orphaning ten years later, when Ivor had made an abrupt political right turn, alienating not only his former readership and employers at the *Gate*, but also the impeccably left-wing daughter that he had raised in what had, until then, been his ideological image.

Over the months of hard work, Danielle had transformed. Her family doctor had put her on a regimen of SSRIs—Danielle had asked Annick what she thought of antidepressants, and Annick had done what she always did in that situation: she pled agnosticism. She wasn't a psychiatrist, she was a psychologist, and it wasn't her role, right or inclination to prescribe or proscribe any type of pills; she'd seen them work before, she'd seen them not work. Danielle had had a difficult time adjusting to the new prescription, but once the meds had attained therapeutic levels in her bloodstream, the combination with Annick's cognitive behavioural therapy had been seemingly unstoppable.

"Your job," Annick explained to her, "is to acknowledge where you're at, and to figure out what kind of goals you can set for yourself that are at exactly the sweet spot—realistic enough to be doable, and enough of a challenge to give you a sense of accomplishment. Some days, that's going to be waking up and having a shower. That's it. But then, once you know that you can do that, the next day it's a shower and you floss. And that's how you get back." And Danielle had. Or at least, that's what Annick had thought until today's phone call.

No, that wasn't fair—Danielle *had* gotten better. The wild swings in weight, the irregular sleeping, the mercurial moods and recriminations: all of that had abated. She would still complain about the comedy industry, with its creeps and its unfairnesses, but now she was winsomely sarcastic about it, cutting; she was above it, no longer equating it with her self-worth. She'd been hired by the Rossi campaign a few months ago to write jokes for his speeches and his social media posts, and though the candidate was well to her right political-ly—"Rossi's a centrist social democrat, basically a sellout, but at least he's pretty hot," she had put it when she was hired— Danielle had enjoyed the work, and seemed to punch through into a whole new level of happiness and self-satisfaction dur-ing the long months of the campaign. A few weeks in, she had begun a romantic relationship with a man in the campaign, though she never said much beyond that. It all seemed to have energized her and filled her with life. But the cop, Mann, had barely hidden her lack of respect for Annick's profes-sional acumen when she had questioned the suicide.

"Was there a date on the suicide note?" Annick had asked.

"I really couldn't say, I don't think so. But that's not really how suicides work, Doctor," Mann had said. "It's not an email."

Annick turned as she heard the key in the door, and the broad smile on Philip's face disappeared instantly as he looked up and saw the look on hers.

"Uh, hey."

"Where were you? I sent you like five texts."

"But I told you—I was having drinks with Tony Chow."

Annick sighed and shook her head. "Right. I'm sorry. I forgot. I'm sorry, I didn't mean to bite your head off."

"Are you okay?"

She looked at him and shook her head again.

"Is it anything you can talk to me about?"

She shook her head one last time. Philip crossed the condo in impossibly few steps and took her into his arms. Annick buried her head against his neck, and Philip twisted to kiss the crown of her head.

"How's Tony?"

"You know how it is. It's the same whenever I see guys from those days," he said, pulling away from her and walking to the kitchen counter, where he kept a pitcher of water so that he could drink it, as he always had growing up, at room temperature. "He wants to spend half the time proving to me how much he's changed, what a good boy he is, like it's a goddamn job interview."

"And the other half?"

"The other half it's just the opposite, like he's trying to prove to himself how tough he'll always be. Reminiscing about shitkickings, the time we pulled a knife on this one, the time we pulled a gun on that one. Just bullshit."

"Wait, we? With a gun?"

Philip grimaced. "No, sorry. No, I never had a gun. That was his story."

"Right, but a knife."

Philip shrugged, drank his water and looked at Annick expectantly. That they had both come up much tougher than most of the yuppie professionals who surrounded them, in their current lives as a psychologist and a science writer, was part of what attracted them to each other and kept them together. And there were stories from Philip's outlaw late adolescence and young adulthood that, on the right night and in the right lighting, could even work a sort of aphrodisiacal magic for Annick. But tonight wasn't that kind of night, and mid-November wasn't letting in that kind of lighting. This was one of those moments when it felt, instead, like Philip's past was something sharp that she had stepped on, in the dark.

"What do you want me to say?" he asked finally.

"Nothing," she said, lifting her shoulders. "I just—"

"What?"

"Nothing."

"No, you just what?"

"It's nothing. I don't know, life's funny, that's all. One day, maybe, I mean who knows—maybe we'll have a kid, and maybe one day . . ."

"Jesus, maybe one day what?"

"I don't know! If it's a boy, maybe he'll think that's what he's supposed to be like. Or a girl. And she might think that's what boys are supposed to be like. Or I don't know. Maybe they would be scared."

"Annick, why the fuck would I tell a kid any of these stories?"

"Oh my God, Philip, are you joking? What do I do for a living? You think families can control every part of which stories get handed down?

"It was a long time ago, alright? I can't change what happened in the past."

"No, I know. I know you can't, *trésor*. I'm sorry." Annick gave a soft smile. "You told me Einstein said there was no past, present or future."

"Fuck," he said, rolling his eyes. "God save me from the people who learn one isolated thing about science."

"Easy. I'm a psychologist, okay? Don't talk to me like I'm some fucking aromatherapist."

"Fine," Philip said, refilling his glass of water. "I'm sorry."

Annick watched as Philip drank his second glass.

"Why are you so thirsty?"

Philip gave another surly shrug. "We had poutine. Probably not up to your Montréal standards. It was salty as hell. I don't know. I had some beers, too. I don't want to be hungover tomorrow."

"Okay. So how's Tony otherwise? He still at that dealership on the way to the airport?"

"He's working for Albion Cross."

"Woah, the developers?"

"Yeah, so he's still a criminal," Philip said, pulling a cold, sticky chicken adobo drumstick from a Tupperware in the fridge and ripping the meat off of it with his teeth in one tear. "You want to watch a movie? I'm going to put on some sweats."

"Sure," Annick said, turning again to stare out at Coal Harbour, now too dark to make out in detail.

6

*i'm sorry i got weird last mon coeur. trouble
on the dark side of the moon. forgive me?*

The "dark side of the moon" had become Philip and
Annick's shorthand, over recent months, for the parts of
their lives cut off to the other. If Annick was troubled by
something she couldn't keep hermetically sealed inside her
work life, but likewise couldn't explain to Philip without vio-
lating patient confidentiality, it would explain her irritability,
or curtness, or absent-mindedness. Philip would know to cut
her some slack. He, likewise, could make use of the system
if he had to protect a source for one of his stories, though
perhaps unsurprisingly the issue didn't come up so much in
the field of science reporting, where Philip was just as likely
to be filing a story on the literal dark side of the actual moon.

When Annick had noticed, at the beginning of the week,
that this particular day of appointments wouldn't get prop-
erly underway until eleven a.m., she'd allowed herself the
girlish fantasy of a slow, lazy morning, forestalling her entry
into the cold, grey damp until the last possible moments.
Instead, she'd arrived early, just a few minutes after Cedric,
and begun poring over her notes from past sessions with

Danielle, to see if it were possible—of course it was possible; it was always possible—that she'd missed something.

Her phone vibrated.

It's fine. We can talk about it later if you want. I don't like having stuff from the past that I have *never* hidden thrown in my face. Have always been straight up with you.

Annick sighed; she didn't know what she'd expected to accomplish with the text, but this certainly hadn't been it. They had sat through the previous evening's movie with chilly indifference, towards it and each other, going to bed at different times. She let out a deep and dispirited exhalation, and set to writing what she hoped was a contrite but dignified response. But she was interrupted by the shrill double-ring of the phone on her desk.

"Hi, Marcel."

"Hello, Dr. Boudreau," answered Marcel, with the unflagging professionalism he brought to all of the clinic's incoming and outgoing communication. "There is a Mr. MacFadden here at the front who would like to see you? He says that he does not have an appointment."

"No," Annick said, her heart picking up, "no, he doesn't. It's fine, send him down. Thanks, Marcel."

Annick imagined that she could hear Marcel beginning to direct the visitor down the corridor towards her office as she was hanging up the phone, and that she was picking up the tail end of the directions *viva voce* as she stood and opened her door to welcome him. At the end of the short hallway, turning the corner a few yards from her office, came a white man in his late sixties, wearing a mismatched denim shirt and jeans and a Gore-Tex jacket from the days of their pure and hideous utility, before they were created as design objects.

Still walking towards her from the hallway, the man croaked a question at her, somehow with a heavy valence of confidence despite its being a question: "You're the shrink? Boudreau?"

"I'm Dr. Boudreau."

"Ivor MacFadden," he said, then gave a wet cough that could have been a smoker's cough or could have been a man trying not to cry. Then, with the same perfectly gruff modulation, he added: "I'm trying to find my daughter."

"Why don't you come into my office, Mr. MacFadden?"

"Ivor."

"Annick."

Ivor nodded stiffly and followed Annick into the office, taking in the details of the room with a journalist's reflexive curiosity as he sat down in the chair where Danielle had sat the previous week.

MacFadden gave a vague, all-purpose nod, but Annick wasn't sure how she was meant to interpret it because his face seemed to be drawn into something like a permanent squint.

"Can I get you anything, Ivor? A glass of water or a cup of coffee, tea?"

"Too early in the day to drink anything useful."

"Okay," Annick said, smiling softly.

Ivor wiped his face with both of his large hands and stared at Annick. It was always an interesting thing when very beautiful women looked a great deal like their fathers. If one knew the father first, it was usually considered at least a little funny, if not slightly unfortunate for the poor girl. But when Annick and Philip had watched *12 Angry Men*, their first sustained exposure to Peter Fonda, neither could get over how pretty he looked, owing to his strong resemblance to Jane. Annick brought the same daughter-first sensibility to Ivor's features, and saw the girl's loveliness cast back a generation underneath the silver beard and wild eyebrows of the father, in his cheekbones and on the bridge of his nose, the large and intelligent eyes. Ivor MacFadden had been a Vancouver legend—not a founding member of Greenpeace, but a fellow traveller and its bard; an editorialist but always, also, a shoe-leather reporter. He had exposed governments municipal and provincial, brought low federal cabinet ministers, and the deep moral assurance of those years was still written into the lines of his face.

"They said my daughter killed herself."

"I got a phone call from the VPD yesterday telling me that that was their assumption. It was an awful call to get—I can't imagine how much worse it was for you. I'm so sorry."

"They found a suicide note."

Annick gave the kind of nod that could have been a confirmation, or just empathetic listening. Ivor wasn't put off by the tactic.

"I say they found a suicide note."

"Yes, I heard you."

"What do you make of that?"

"I can't imagine how difficult this must be. But I—it would be inappropriate for me, and I really have no grounds, for speculating on an open police investigation."

"Open! Open and shut. Girl's reported missing by the old lady on the main floor who brings up the mail, they find old empty bottles of antidepressants in the suite, they find a suicide note, how much sniffing around do you think they keep doing after that?"

"I don't know," Annick answered, entirely honestly.

"Sure. I'll bet there's a lot you don't know. Otherwise, how else does a young woman end up coming in here, giving you however many months of her time, however many hundreds of her dollars, and still somehow, she's in a state of popping pills and leaving suicide notes?"

"Mr. MacFadden, I can't imagine the pain you must be feeling at the moment. I would ask you, though, to address yourself to that pain, rather than coming into my office and impugning not only my work, but also your daughter, from a position of spectacularly splendid ignorance. Is that clear?"

Annick had seen that look before: the look that appears when two people, meeting in a professional context, bite down on the hard kernel of shared blue-collar mettle. Far from angering or alienating MacFadden, Annick's response had clearly passed some sort of smell test for him.

"But you don't think she killed herself."

"Listen, I'm not—"

"Don't worry about the confidentiality song and dance, I'm still the goddamn next of kin, for Chrissakes. So we don't talk, well—okay. That's not my choice. I'm still her goddamn father and the institutions of Western liberal democracy haven't entirely eroded into the soup of postmodern relativist whims *just yet*, and so as the father of a missing young woman, presumed dead by suicide, I'm still entitled to some information, from the police department if not from the inviolable spiral-ring notebook of some psychiatrist. Alright?"

"Actually, I'm a psychologist."

"Same thing."

"Not really, no."

Ivor sighed loudly. "The cops told me that you said you didn't think she'd killed herself." After pronouncing what he knew, and how he knew it, a neediness shifted into MacFadden's body language. The heel of his left foot began bouncing, and his chin dropped slightly, and Annick realized now that this was the closest Ivor MacFadden could bring himself to pleading. "Is that true? You don't think my daughter's dead?"

Annick shook her head in a way that could have been a no, or could have been more empathetic listening, as she calculated the ethical parameters of the situation. Whether or not they were estranged, MacFadden was right: he was Danielle's next of kin. Danielle had even listed him as such with the clinic. Given the context, Annick saw no reason why she couldn't confirm what the police had already told him.

"In my opinion, as I told the police—I had no reason to believe, from my most recent interactions with Danielle, that there was any imminent threat of self-harm." Annick looked at his pleading eyes, so much like his daughter's only filled with fear and dread and searching hope, and spoke again before she realized she was adding anything. "In fact, quite the opposite."

Ivor's facial expression didn't change, but he sat nodding for several seconds, then shot up out of the chair and stepped towards the door.

"Thank you," he said without turning. "I'll let you know if I need any help finding my daughter."

7

IN THE TWELVE MINUTES' walk along the harbour-front promenade from the SkyTrain station to the condo tower, Annick's jeans had soaked halfway up her calves with rainwater. There were still those who insisted on using umbrellas against the city's pervading late-autumn wetness, which seemed, to her, to make as much sense as locking the skylight windows against burglars and then leaving all the doors propped open. There was no direction from which the cold wet wouldn't hit you, and the only options seemed to be either to dress in the top-to-tail waterproofing of the lobster fishermen in her home province, or else to surrender to a certain degree of discomfort. The years that Annick had spent living in Montréal, as a university student, had inoculated her against committing any of the thousand and one crimes against style that Vancouverites performed every day, the most visible holdover from the city's still-recent years as a provincial backwater. But when faced with the pounding precipitation of a rainforest without most of its trees, even the most sophisticated Montrealers would have to surrender to the necessity of a waterproof jacket, and the hood of Annick's little red number—a vain attempt to rage against the colourlessness of the rainy season—was pulled tight against the sides of her face, blocking out the world. For a quarter of the year, Vancouver was a city with no peripheral vision.

Entering the condo elevator, Annick smiled and nodded at a middle-aged neighbour riding up bone dry from the parkade and received, in exchange, a scandalized head-to-toe appraisal of her dripping wetness. Being both unwilling and unable to do a full-body canine shake before entering the lobby, Annick shrugged, waved her fob and pressed the button for her floor.

As she entered the condominium, Annick was surprised to find several of the lights on, and Philip's work shoes at the door, but no Philip.

"*Mon coeur*? Philip?" she called out into the empty flat, before realizing that he must have gone downstairs to the condo gym.

Back in the elevator, Annick stared with shame at the puddle she'd left, and when a neighbour from two floors down entered the car, saying "Oh, yuck!" Annick nodded meekly and offered a pained "Some people!" in reply.

In less than two months, when the new year would officially begin, the condo gym would be chock-a-block for six or seven weeks, and it would be nearly impossible to move for all the earnest self-improvement and physical renewal taking place. But in these last languid, chubby months of the old year, Philip had the space to himself. Far from a monastic calm, though, his solitude instead provided the context for a hysterical flurry of aggressive sounds and kinetic noise; on his own, Philip felt free to let loose, and was currently doing so onto the Everlast heavy bag hanging from the ceiling. The sonic intensity of the punching bag had occasionally, in point of fact, become a matter of contention at various strata council meetings. Annick and Philip had rolled their eyes at the genteel aristocrats among their neighbours who couldn't handle the noise the bag made within the confines of the gym (for the two months of the year when they used it), but listening now to the thick chains dancing and bouncing, and Philip's every pounding thud into the canvas accompanied by a sharp, punching exhalation of breath, she had to admit that there was something unsettling about it. Despite it, or because of it, Annick was fixated.

As she approached the corner where Philip was punching, watching from behind as his shoulders worked against the bag, Annick began to wonder how she could signal to him that she was there without shocking him into a heart attack. She could hear the music blaring through his headphones even from a few metres back. At the same time, she worried that if she laid a hand on his shoulder in the midst of his violent aerobic windmilling against the punching bag, he might turn and strike her purely from instinct. As she was wondering what to do, Philip suddenly stopped, putting his hand out to still the bag, and turned to her.

"Hey," he said.

Annick didn't know what to say. "How—you knew I was here?"

"Yes."

"How?"

Philip smiled, then laughed. He pointed at the mirrored wall he'd been working against. Annick fell down laughing, sitting hard on a workout bench.

"Man, they were just giving away PhDs the day you got yours, huh?"

"Careful now."

"Yeah? What's so good about careful?"

"Because, if you aren't, you might thoughtlessly say something that hurts someone you love very, very much. Even if it was the furthest thing from your mind."

"Yeah?" Philip arched an eyebrow, then bent to grab his water bottle, taking a pull. "How would that make me feel?"

"Very, very, sorry."

Philip nodded. "Well, you'll have a chance to repay your debt to society."

"Me? I thought we were talking about you."

"Ah. Okay."

"But for argument's sake, if I did have a debt to repay to society—how do you see me paying that back? Hypothetically."

"We're having dinner with Tony Chow and his girlfriend tomorrow night. And there's nothing hypothetical about it."

Annick let out an involuntary, pained breath. "That is both cruel and unusual."

But Philip's mind was already on to other things. "Those clothes are pretty wet, eh?"

"They are, yes."

"I might even use the word 'clingy.'"

"Takes one to know one."

They stared at each other for a moment longer, smiling, before Philip reached his hand out and jerked his head towards the sauna in the corner of the gym. "Let's go have a quick sweat."

"Is the sauna on?"

"Not yet. But they get hot pretty fast."

Annick and Philip broke by-law 26(f), page 32 of the strata agreement. But whoever entered the elevator on her way back up to the condo, Annick greeted them with a very large and sincere smile.

✳

Annick stood in front of the open fridge, running her finger along the thin line of skin between the hem of her T-shirt and the band of her pyjama bottoms. Warmed over by a shower just a few degrees shy of scalding, she was now bone dry for the first time that day, for what felt like the first time in weeks, and the chill of the refrigerator felt puny before the might and permanence of her comfortable warmth. Similarly, as she turned back towards the floor-to-ceiling view of the grey wet chill outside, fortified by a palmful of cranberry-bison pepperoni sticks and fresh memories of post-coital shuddering, Annick felt a rush of empowerment over the desolate gloominess that encircled her from all sides, until she realized that she hadn't thought about Danielle for an hour and a half.

You couldn't screw your way out of depression, but, as her mentor Dr. Conte had also told her, "a healthy lay has never set anyone's head back." Before Danielle had begun dating her mystery man on the Rossi campaign team, things had already been progressing with regard to her mood and her outlook for weeks, if not months. She had been exercising and beginning to regularize her sleep; the new writing job had been a shot in the arm and the SSRIS prescribed by Dr. Tsong had seemed to be a good fit after some initial difficulties from side effects—in this she had been lucky, as SSRIS were temperamental and it often took a few tries to find the best prescription for a particular individual. But the day she had told Dr. Boudreau about the new relationship, she had been very nearly giddy, with an almost slumber party energy very out of keeping with her typical air of detached cool.

"So, uh . . . *I met a boy* . . ." she had said in a giggling sing-song, her cheeks reddening as she pinched her forehead in embarrassment.

"Well, that's nice—who is he? Where did you guys meet?"

The war between a desperate desire to share and the need to keep a secret had been immediately in evidence, written in every feature of the patient's smiling face. Finally, biting her full bottom lip and shaking her long ponytail, Danielle had given a smiling wince and said, "I'm not supposed to say. It's delicate, because we met through the campaign. I promised him. Even you."

Dr. Boudreau had raised both hands in the air in mock surrender. "Hey, it's none of my business what his name is—I'm happy if you're happy."

"I'm happy. Very happy."

"Good. And just for the record, even if you had accidentally spilled the beans—you know everything you say in here is completely confidential."

"I know, I know," she had replied, no longer making any effort to conceal either her joy or her embarrassment. "But he made me swear."

Annick was a doctor, but she was also a human being, and so it had been hard not to speculate as to who on the campaign the inamorato might have been. It could, of course, have been any low-level phone-bank volunteer or community outreach organizer, in which case the name wouldn't have meant anything to Annick anyway. But she doubted it.

To begin with, Danielle wasn't the kind of woman approached by phone-bank volunteers. These kinds of things weren't hard and fast rules, of course, but there were patterns. Annick herself, for instance, knew that she was very cute; she wouldn't have carried off a shaved head so confidently for all those months if she weren't. But she also knew that she was cute in a short and soft-edged way that men on the whole—in ways sometimes flattering, sometimes deeply irritating—found accessible if not outright inviting. Danielle, on the other hand, with her height and her cinematic features, bore a kind of mythical beauty that instantly struck whole classes of men, rightly or wrongly, as unattainable. Women like Danielle were approached by only the swaggering and confident, obnoxious or oblivious. Of course only someone nearish the top of the campaign infrastructure would have needed to ask Danielle to keep their relationship a secret; but Annick also figured no one else would have had the guts to ask her out in the first place.

Even still, Danielle was smart enough to know that whatever she had told Dr. Boudreau would have stayed safely within the walls of the office, and so it seemed as though there had to be an added reason for the secrecy. For whatever reason, she must have been embarrassed by the identity of her campaign boyfriend. And for all those reasons, Annick had secretly suspected that the mystery man had to be the campaign consultant–strategist guru, Kingsley Davis.

Still not quite forty-five years old, Davis's last big accomplishment before the Vancouver election had been to return the Ontario Liberal Party to a majority government after a generation scattered to the four winds of the country's most populous province; before that, he had consulted on successful local campaigns by federal candidates for the New Democratic Party. Rather than running from it as a liability, Davis leaned into this partisan promiscuity as a strength, committing himself only and entirely to the principle of "helping progressives win elected office in Canada, period." Tall, lean, with reddish-brown hair and see-through-frame glasses, Davis was the kind of guy who was never clean-shaven but also never had a beard. After having first met him, Danielle had described him by saying: "He's not a douchebag—he's like the giant bag that many douchebags are stored in." Annick thought that if she had delivered a line that devastating, and then started dating the guy, she'd probably keep it under wraps too.

Annick dropped onto the sectional in front of the TV as though it were a fainting couch and gnawed at the pepperoni sticks as she navigated with the remote control, wondering what she would watch and whether this was dinner. She fought against any further thoughts about Danielle or her sad, estranged father, knowing that for the time being she had no option but to wait for more information. Annick clicked onto a baking show that she already seen, and sank farther into the couch, eyeing her cell phone on the coffee table and considering whether she could order something up, or if they'd already eaten out too many times that week.

Without thinking about it too much, or stopping to consider whether it was morbid or invasive, Annick opened YouTube with the remote, and pecked out the words "DANIELLE MACFADDEN STAND-UP" one letter at a time. A high-quality video of Danielle, standing next to a stool and dressed down exquisitely in an obscure concert T-shirt and dowdy cardigan with her hair in a high ponytail, appeared, having previously been viewed several thousand times. She looked perfect despite, or because of, all of her efforts to draw attention towards her jokes, and Annick silently promised she wouldn't subject herself to reading any of the comments. She pressed play, and as the video began, the audience was already in the middle of a laugh.

"I guess I would describe myself as sort of a classic daddy's girl, you know? Because my mom's dead." The first big laugh popped, much louder than the minority of piteous groans. "Like a lot of dads, mine had a lot of goofy nicknames for me. Is that, like—for the girls in the audience, was that your experience?" Hoots of agreement and recognition. "Okay good. I didn't want to, like, colonize you with *my* nickname truth." More giggles. "Subconsciously I think a lot of dads give their daughters goofy nicknames as like a way of inoculating us against being sexualized by a society that privileges the male gaze, you know? Like, 'I don't care if you're in college, nobody wants to do anal with *Scooter.*'" Big laughs and applause, along with wails of performative disapproval. "A lot of you guys didn't feel good about that joke. Even though in that hypothetical scenario, no one did anything developmentally inappropriate." Danielle smiled at someone in the audience in a way that, Annick imagined, must have made them glow for days. "I think it's easier for dads to give kids stupid nicknames than it is for moms because women carry the babies for nine fucking months and it's just, like, way harder to be chill about it after that kind of commitment. 'This is my daughter Jennifer.' 'Oh cool, can I just call her Jenny Benny?' 'Yeah, no problem. *After* you have carried her on your torso giving her half of every meal for three full seasons, okay? You make it from one equinox to another living with her as a symbiotic hernia and *Jenny Benny*'s all yours, cool?' I feel like the entire asymmetry of reproduction can be summed up in the fact that I was literally born with eggs already in my ovaries, whereas my boyfriend's nuts started making sperm ten minutes before we lit the incense. Okay, obviously I'm exaggerating a little bit to make a point. He has a Glade air freshener."

The keys jangled in the lock, and Annick realized that she had tears running down her cheeks. She sat up abruptly, not knowing if she'd been laughing or crying, and wiped her face roughly with the cuff of her sleeve. Philip came in, still breathing heavily from the rest of his post-sauna workout. He pulled the headphones from his ears, the music still blaring for a second before it died, before calling out,

"Hey! You wanna order something for dinner?"

"Sure," she said, turning off the TV. "I was going to make something, but I guess we could if you want."

"Sweet. I'm gonna hop in the shower, Bean."

Annick rolled her eyes and smiled. *Bean.* Speaking of dumb pet names; at least she knew that they were now fully reconciled. *Bean* was one of those nauseating nicknames which evolved along the labyrinthine pathways taken by a couple's life together, almost impossible to retrace for an outsider: affectionately teasing his white francophone beloved, Philip had first started calling Annick "French Vanilla," which had then contracted to simply "Vanilla," before re-expanding to "Vanilla Bean," until settling finally, and economically, on *Bean*.

As she heard the shower running, and watched one of the baking show contestants pouring, coincidentally, a teaspoon of vanilla extract into their mixing bowl, Annick smiled and reflected on the fact that love must truly be as powerful as all the singers and poets insist, given the idiotic diminutives we allow ourselves to be called by in its name. Then she gasped, and shot up in her seat.

"'Berto.'"

8

SITTING AT HER DESK after the last of her patients had left for the day, staring at the on-screen notes from her sessions with Danielle, Annick reached her hand up behind her neck, digging the ends of her fingers into the knot where her shoulders began, and tried to trick herself into thinking she was being massaged.

The previous evening's epiphany that, at some point in Danielle's stories about the work she was doing on the mayoral campaign, the candidate had gone from "Rossi" to "Berto"—without even a stop at the intimate way station of "Alberto," the man's actual Christian name—was admittedly a slim reed to cling to. But the notes from their sessions did reveal an evolution, not only in Danielle's appellation for the mayoral candidate but also in her esteem for him more generally.

The initial contact between Danielle and the Rossi camp had come through a mutual friend of hers and of Tavleen Dosanjh, Rossi's campaign manager, the youthful and glamorous operative who was legendary despite, or in part because of, her years. Dosanjh had gone to the same university as Danielle at the same time, though the two women had known each other only vaguely in their time on campus. But as Danielle's reputation as a comic, and Tavleen's as a serious politico, had grown, neither had had to make too much of an effort to stay informed of the other's trajectory. When Tavleen had casually mentioned the liability of her candidate's oratory woodenness to Daphne Rosario, herself a committed amateur comic who had been an undergraduate with both women—but failed to escape the university and was now nearly finished a PhD, Daphne had offered to set up drinks.

The problem was that Rossi was invariably magnetic in unstructured, off-the-cuff interactions with the media and public, or could learn and deliver a formal speech that had been prepared for him down to the comma and semi-colon, but something seemingly innate and insurmountable in his wiring prevented him from performing any combination of both things at once. Tavleen asked Danielle to make herself available, for an hourly rate, to go through prepared speeches doing "punch-up" work: looking for opportunities to lighten things here and there, offering suggestions for jokes that the candidate could slip into his prepared remarks as though they were merely an extension of his charming patter. She couldn't tell anyone that she had written the jokes, any more than the other speechwriters could or would take any credit for the ideas in them, and that had been fine by Danielle, who'd been embarrassed to take the job and likely wouldn't have if the money hadn't been as good as it was. And the way the gig had been presented, she would never have to be at the office or present for campaign events, and might not even meet Rossi face to face.

But the first speech she punched up was Rossi's address to the Vancouver Trade & Commerce Committee, a kennel of purebred foxhounds for whom the East Van trade union leader's otherwise impeccably moderate credentials came off instead like the heavy musk of Bolshevism. Rossi's speech to the hostile crowd was as part of a traditional end-of-week luncheon gathering named, without irony or evident playfulness, Free Market Friday. Despite Rossi alone in enemy territory, Danielle suggested that he lean into the act, even open with it:

"I have to admit that this is my first Free Market Friday, and I don't know if I'm cut out for it. I asked for a slot on Theoretical Marxism Thursday, but they never got back to me." The line had absolutely killed. The next day, in the column of Don Chalmers, lead political reporter for the *Vancouver Chronicle*, it and no less than three other lines Danielle had written were quoted word for word. It was at that point, apparently, that Rossi had insisted on meeting her.

When Danielle had relayed the story to Dr. Boudreau, it had been with a sort of sheepish triumphalism. As a joke writer, she couldn't deny the pride that came from slaying a crowd, even when she was once removed from the action. But she had been quick to insist to her therapist, upon being hired and for the first few weeks of work on the campaign, that Rossi was not the kind of candidate she could get excited about. He was too middle-of-the-road, too timid, too willing to keep the city's troughs open to the same powerful interests who'd always sidled up to them, leaving scant room for anybody else. Rossi was the kind of candidate, she explained, whom she might feel some minor relief upon discovering had won over a more openly hateful or rapacious option, but he wasn't special enough that she felt she had any skin in the game.

Over the weeks, though, that had seemed to change. Not explicitly, but sideways. Little things, like the use of "we" in reference to the campaign, or visceral frustration when Rossi opted not to use insult lines that Danielle had written against the other candidates. And perhaps most significantly, the slippage from Rossi to Berto.

Annick sighed and looked at her clock. She was not looking forward to dinner with Tony Chow and his girlfriend, but she had made a promise to Philip, and, at the very least, they were dining at Mykonos, on Fraser Street, which was in Annick's experience the first Greek restaurant in Vancouver to realize that one well-prepared entrée on its own, à la carte, was better than a plate filled with seven mediocre sides. She shut off her computer and tried to give her neck another amateur chiropractic pull. She settled for releasing a slow, tired moan.

She stood and took her rain jacket from the wooden coat rack that she had giggled at when Philip gave to her but which both she and her patients had come to appreciate not only for its beauty but also for its function. As she turned to slip her arm down her coat sleeve, she stared into her empty patient chair and, despite the many people who had filled it since he'd sat there, thought of Ivor MacFadden. She sat back down in her seat and fixated on the chair, willing herself somehow to understand.

If her patient was dead by suicide, Annick wanted to know; she would be devastated, but she understood, rationally, that it wouldn't be the end for her. It was true that she had never lost a patient this way, but of course she had always worked with the implicit understanding that it was a possibility. She couldn't reduce it to the glib patness of a phrase like "occupational hazard," not least because she wasn't the primary victim—but it was nevertheless a particular emotional risk that came with the kind of work she did. She could never have prepared for the specific pain of an actual case, but she had, even if only subconsciously, girded herself against the possibility in general.

But what about a parent? A father who long ago lost his wife, presented now with the possibility that his daughter, too, is irretrievably gone?

Annick ran the palm of her hand in a circle over her scalp four, five, six times. She thought of her father, Roméo, on the other side of the country; Vancouver to Halifax was twice the distance from London to Moscow, and yet somehow they entertained the idea that they were still in the same country. She thought of the worst days of his colon cancer, his pale mottled skin as tight to his bones as the plastic wrap on the moose meat he would come home with from New Brunswick when she was a girl, when he was younger, healthier, laughing and red-cheeked. Annick had never been a crier but her trip back East to help her mother tend to her sick father had changed that part of her, opened it up. At night, once both her parents were sleeping, Annick would sit on the bed in her old room and heave luxurious sobs up out of her stomach, the soles of her feet. And yet if the worst had happened, if she had lost Roméo—that was the way things were *supposed* to go. If everything went absolutely right she would still, one day, bury her father. She shuddered against the thought of the other order of things, the unnatural way. The idea of a parent losing their child seemed like one of those pains so enormous, of such metaphysical proportions, that it might make one think twice about risking even its possibility.

She picked up the phone and dialled. It took three rings for him to answer.

"*Oui, âllo?*"

"*Papa?*"

"*Salut, beauté!* That's a nice surprise in the middle of the week from my busy girl!"

"Oh, stop it."

"So—who died?"

9

JUST AS ANNICK pulled the car-share vehicle up in front of Mykonos, another car was leaving a parallel space directly outside the front door. She had a colleague, a full-bodied Iraqi-Kurdish dialectical-behavioural therapist based in Calgary, who referred to such serendipities joyfully as "fat man parking," but though the phrase had a kind of irresistibility to it, Annick felt forbidden from using it not so much by gender expression as by BMI. She looked at the dashboard clock and saw that she was only a few minutes late for dinner; she looked at the empty cup holder and squinted, trying to remember if she'd had a travel mug with her.

Mykonos was done entirely in timeless Cobalt blue, with white accents and both images of pottery and bits of the real stuff to drive home the Hellenism. Early-'90s hip hop was piped loudly through the restaurant's speakers, and Annick reflected that neither of these aesthetic elements would ever go stale. She smiled and nodded at a beautiful young server carrying what appeared to be a tray of octopus, then saw Philip waving her in from a booth in the middle of the restaurant's far wall.

"Hi, sorry I'm late everybody," Annick said as Philip stood and pecked her on the cheek. "Wow, Tony, you're clearly a good influence. Feels like only yesterday I couldn't get my fella to stand like a gentleman when I arrived to table."

"First time anyone's accused me of being a good influence on Phil," Tony laughed, and his girlfriend pinched the arm that was swelling under his suit jacket.

Annick noticed immediately that the adolescent tough guy was far less submerged in the adult Tony than he was in the adult Philip. Tony Chow did not come across as a man whom many people argued with about parking spaces, or grocery store line-up placement. Annick knew that to barely stuff one's heaving muscles into the narrow confines of an otherwise impeccable suit was a favoured look among some of the Downtown set, but on Tony, the style had the added dimension of a bruiser; he was dressed in such a way that he could be crooning a set onstage at a jazz club, but if there were any trouble in the crowd, he would also be the one hurling drunks headfirst into the alleyway. He was bald, but clearly by choice, with an immaculately tended pencil moustache and three-inch goatee. His girlfriend, Kimberley, was dressed in expensive but uninteresting clothing, and had a face that was pretty but severe, with small green eyes, and her red hair was shining such that Annick had to check to see if she was sitting underneath one of the track lighting lamps.

"The psychiatrist is late! I blame childhood trauma," said Tony, smiling, pointing at Annick's head.

"Stop it!" said Kimberley, slapping him. She gawped, revealing dizzyingly perfect teeth, and Annick smirked.

"Psychologist. Have you guys ordered anything yet?"

"Only drinks," said Philip, just as the waiter arrived with two tall glasses of local microbrew beer for him and Tony, and a ginger ale for Kimberley.

"Can I get you anything?" the waiter asked Annick.

"You know what, we'll grab some appies for the table to start. Make it the kontosouvli, two orders of the octopus and a lamb sausage, just bring 'em as they're ready."

"Sure," said the waiter.

"And I'll have a white wine, please." Annick added. "Just something dry. Thank you." She turned to the table. "Well, nothing worse than someone who shows up late and expects a recap on what they missed—but imagining, for a moment, that I were that self-centred . . ."

"Tony was just telling me about his boss's vacation place. Traverso . . .? No, what did you say it was called?"

Tony smiled, and articulated carefully with a vicarious pride. "Tramonto Sopra Vesuvio."

"Ooh," said Annick, half-sincerely impressed. "Rich people don't name a place unless it's serious. Italy, I assume?"

Tony shook his head, still smiling. "Nope, Salt Spring Island."

"Oh, really? I love Salt Spring. It's just beautiful over there. So peaceful—the trees, the water. Gorgeous."

"Well, like I said to Philly," Tony continued, "we're actually headed over there; I'm bringing Kimmy. But next time you guys gotta come. Place is a palace. Here, actually," he said, fishing his phone from his pocket, "do you have AirDrop on? I'm gonna send you a couple of these pictures."

Philip, who Annick knew would have no interest whatsoever in seeing Miles Truscott's palatial chalet, gamely indulged his friend, retrieving his own phone and making moon eyes at what he saw.

"Woah, man."

Philip turned his screen towards Annick, letting her flip through the pictures with the tip of her index finger as she shook her head and affected a look of enthusiasm. Several shots of an immense gas-range kitchen, with magazine-perfect copper pots hung with European-style utilitarian whimsy above a massive granite island, transitioned into shots of a soaring living room sheltered by thick, handsome beams and warmed by a rough-hewn stone fireplace; there were shots of a shower with four heads and a mahogany snooker table underneath what looked, to Annick, like a large Stan Douglas photograph mounted and carefully lit on the wall. She shook her head and grinned ironically.

"Some people and their money, eh?"

"Was I lying? Nuts, right? Six bedrooms, games room, tennis court, home theatre, Jacuzzi, sauna . . ."

"I like saunas," said Annick.

As the dinner progressed, Tony got bigger and bigger, and Annick tried to watch, out of the corner of her eye, to see what it did to Philip. She was the only one at the table, clearly, who didn't know the stories being told off by heart: Philip and Tony from having been there, and Kimberley from having sat through who knew how many rehearsals and iterations and expansions of each. The menace and criminality of each anecdote had been front-loaded, usually leading to some comically ironic upshot. Philip winced and laughed as Tony set out in epic set pieces the meandering story of a fistfight in an East Side greasy spoon, whose grateful manager later thanked them for providing a diversion from the spot kitchen inspection he never would have passed. Philip buried his face in his hands as Tony, working around a mouthful of pita and smoky *taramosalata*, recounted the tale of a van stolen from a suburban Cineplex parkade, which turned out to have two sleeping poodles on the back bench. And yet none of the stories was being told for Annick's sake, and certainly not for Kimberley's, either. Annick didn't like to make a habit of psychologizing in her off-hours, but people like Tony made it hard not to—the man wore his insecurities like a hazmat suit. Here was a guy who'd been dragged into adulthood kicking and screaming; he'd been a hard man in training then opted for something softer, and for some reason he resented either himself for the decision or everybody else for how he imagined it made them think of him.

But what about her Philip, who *had* wanted to grow up? Who possessed the one trait common to every genuine tough guy Annick had ever known, which was an obliterating indifference as to anyone's opinion about their toughness— the occasional drunken holiday party notwithstanding? As she watched his face she saw a play of genuine tension and contradiction, a now embarrassed, now nostalgic set of alternating smiles, a shaking of his head in disbelief, either at what he used to get up to or else that he was stuck here at dinner. Tony touched a part of Philip that preceded Annick, and so she wasn't quite sure the shape or the weight of it. She ran her hand along the bench to his thigh and squeezed.

"So work must be pretty good, your boss is bringing you out to Xanadu on the Gulf Islands?" Philip asked immediately, as though the spontaneous leg squeeze had been some sort of pre-arranged signal.

Tony shook his head and smiled joylessly, throwing back the last of his second beer. "Fuckin' meltdown, man. You can't say anything, but this Rossi shit is fuckin' Chernobyl. 9/11." He giggled, then his face went serious again. "It's crazy, man."

"I thought Rossi was Mr. Condo?" said Annick. Tony shrugged and shook his head.

"Not on Knight Street he isn't. Not if Satan's Hammer tells him he can't."

"What?" asked Philip, with genuine confusion. Kimberley's eyes followed the conversation from face to face.

"Actually I heard something about this," said Annick, wondering how much of Bonnie's conjecture she ought reasonably to be passing along. "Just, like, a rumour that the reason Rossi walked back the trucking phase-out along Knight was the Hammer and the waterfront stuff."

"Yeah, meanwhile he's leaving everybody else standing along Knight Street with our dicks out," said Tony, angrily wiping his mouth with the back of his hand. "Knight Street without trucking was all set to be the Cambie Street of the East Side."

Annick laughed. "I'll bet."

The look on Tony's face told her immediately that he hadn't been kidding. "I'm not joking, man. That was the marketing pitch. The plans were all ready to go. Albion alone had land assemblies along the corridor worth a hundred million dollars and change. That's the *land* value. Like, now. That's the money they were *starting* with."

"Holy shit," said Philip.

"And now what, instead of sitting on the city's last virgin gold mine, they're going to have to sell that land, throw out all that work, for pennies on the dollar? Fuck that."

"Your bosses must be pissed."

Tony shook his head, smiled. "That's what I thought, but honestly it seems more like fuckin' heartbreak. Miles Truscott, he grew up with Rossi. They go way back."

"Who, Truscott? The cancer bike-a-thon guy? Shit, right—that's who it was! Remember Annick? We saw him the other night at D'Angelo's. He was eating with the mayor."

"Lou Gehrig's."

"What?"

"The bike-a-thon. ALS."

"Right. But what do you mean he grew up with Rossi? He seems like a Shaughnessy, Point Grey type all the way. St. George's."

"No, he is. But him and Rossi were high-school debaters."

Philip smiled. "Got it. So Rossi would go over to the West Side, East Van's conquering hero against the private school boys."

"Wait a minute," said Annick. "This was after the Knight Street backdown, the dinner at D'Angelo's. Why would he be breaking bread with Rossi after all that?"

"No, that's what I'm telling you! They've known each other more than twenty years. With Miles, there's business, and there's friendship, and you don't let one influence the other."

"That's pretty magnanimous," offered Annick. "I have a colleague who might even call it Zen."

"I'd be Zen too if I had six bedrooms and a tennis court on Salt Spring Island," said Philip, and Tony laughed.

The server approached the table once more, holding an empty tray against her hip. "Can I get you guys anything else?"

Annick started, "I think just the—"

"Two more pints of those Magic Mikes, another white wine and another ginger ale."

"I'm just going to have a glass of water, please," said Annick by way of amendment.

"What?" protested Tony. "Come on!"

"No, no, sorry—work night. Plus I'm driving. But you guys go ahead."

The waiter smiled and nodded her head, giving the tray a wiggle of goodbye as she left.

"Party pooper," said Tony.

"Okay, wrap it up," said Philip.

"I'm just joking, you know I'm joking."

"Of course," said Annick. "I just don't like to have more than one glass of wine if I've dropped acid."

"Doctor's orders," added Philip.

"I keep telling you I'm not that kind of doctor."

"Besides," said Philip, "not to point fingers, but I mean, come on, I don't see you ragging on Kimberley for the ginger ales here."

Kimberley smiled proudly, then conspiratorially at Tony.

"Well," said Tony, smiling warmly now himself, "that really *is* doctor's orders."

✤

Annick and Philip rode quietly along the dark and mostly empty wet streets until the Cambie Bridge. As Downtown Vancouver rose up in front of them, on the other side of the pulsing windshield wipers, Philip finally spoke.

"I can't believe Tony Chow is having a goddamn *baby*."

"Maybe it and the mother can learn to speak at the same time."

Philip gave a slow but sincere, beer-roughened laugh. He turned and stared out the passenger window at the rain. "What you said, the other night—about one day, if we have a kid?"

"Love, I'm sorry."

"No, not that. I just mean . . . Do you ever think about having a kid anymore?"

Annick thought about Ivor MacFadden, somewhere in the city, wondering whether his daughter was missing, in danger, or else whether the life he had given her had been so suffocatingly lightless that she had chosen, irrevocably, to withdraw from it. She wondered herself whether she was strong enough to withstand that kind of pain. She wondered whether she could give someone life, knowing how often it could end up feeling like that.

"I don't know," she said. "Now's not really a good time."

"It's never a 'good time,' though."

"No, it isn't."

They rode along in silence, the rain hammering the roof of the car-share vehicle, the windshield wipers mounting a Sisyphean campaign for visibility.

"So," Annick ventured softly, meaning to do it gently and with winsome irony, but already not liking the way it had come out, "do you have the Tony Itch out of your system or is this a new thing? Are you, like, planning to start hanging out with him again regularly?"

Philip shook his head but didn't answer.

"I'm not trying to be a snob—"

"You don't have to. It's coming easy tonight."

"Oh, bullshit. I'm not ragging on him for chewing taffy in the opera box. That tailored sausage-casing shirt he was squeezed into cost more than the suits my father was baptized in, married in and will be buried in combined. Don't give me snob."

"Then what's your problem?"

"He's a bore! And a boor! He is boring, and overbearing, and he doesn't let his girlfriend talk, or anybody else either—"

"You don't —"

"—And I wouldn't be saying any of this if I didn't know you knew it. So I'm just trying to figure out why you'd want to give this guy the time of day? You've outgrown him, Philip."

"You don't outgrow scars. You grow with them, around them. I don't know how else to say it."

"He's a *scar* to you?"

"I'm not saying it right. I had three beers."

"Four."

"Thanks."

Annick checked her blind spot, then began a crawl across several lanes of downtown traffic in anticipation of a turn.

"You can't understand this, the stuff we went through together," Philip said finally.

"Like *what*?" Annick said impatiently.

"He put somebody in a wheelchair because of me," Philip nearly shouted, and Annick instinctively stopped the car. Behind her, cars began honking, and she quickly brought her trembling hands back up to the wheel and put the car back in motion. "Careful," Philip said hoarsely, not meeting her searching eyes. He didn't continue until the car was back up to speed. "It was grade twelve. We were out at a bush party at Deer Lake, out in Burnaby? Way out on a limb. Back in those days, the two big gangs in Burnaby were a big group of white guys and a big group of Spanish guys, Latino. The brown guys, like the Indian kids, they were about evenly split between the whites and the Spanish. We had a couple of buddies, couple Chinese, Korean guys, sort of flying the flag, you know? But they were like—it was like RC Cola trying to flex next to Coke and Pepsi. So a bunch of us drove out to this party for backup. Like a show of force.

"But when we get there, nobody's there from either of the gangs. Maybe a couple guys, but mostly it's just kids getting hammered, making out on the benches . . . it was still light when we got there but it got dark so quick, and I guess I lost track of why we were there.

"I met this girl, she was in grade ten at one of the Burnaby schools, and we started fooling around. We were over behind this, like, work shed or something, and we were, like, going pretty good, so much that I didn't hear these three guys, two white guys and one brown guy, when they came up on us. The girl ran and the three guys just swarmed me, kicked the shit out of me. I didn't even realize what was happening at first—all I could really see was that one of the white guys was super tall, with big ears and a shaved head. I wasn't even sure why they stopped. It was so dark, and I was drunk, and they were laughing. But I just lay there for five, ten minutes. Maybe it was more than that."

"Jesus, Philip. How have you never told me this before?"

"Tony found me. He was looking for me. He helped me up and I told him what happened. I don't think I could've picked the other two guys out of a crowd of four, but that tall, jug-eared fucker, I could spot him halfway across the park, hardly any light. I fingered him for Tony."

Philip paused in his telling and turned to Annick. He gave a short, ironic laugh in disbelief at the memories he was unspooling, at their easy vividness, and Annick squeezed his knee.

"The guy was carrying this drunk girl to a car."

"Oh my God."

"Like, she could barely stand. And I'm watching now, the guy leans her up against the car to get his keys out of his fleece, and Tony just haymakers him in the back of the neck, right at the base of his skull. He slumped as fast as the girl did, both just two sacks of potatoes. But then Tony starts stomping the guy."

"Oh, Jesus."

"It's going on for so long, but I don't want to yell out his name, right? I don't know how to get him to stop. Finally, I shout, 'It's okay!' Tony looks up at me from a hundred feet away like I've walked in on him somewhere, like he's completely forgotten I was there, what he's doing.

"He rushed over to me, doesn't say anything except 'Come on.' We jump in his car and peel off for East Van. We didn't even tell our guys we were leaving. It was a huge story. The kid never walked again. His dad was a big wheel, owned a bunch of restaurants. It was all over everything, the news, but nobody saw anything, and nobody at the park knew Tony."

Annick had parked the car, a few minutes before, across from the entrance to their building, and now they sat watching the water in unbroken waves on the windshield. She shook her head.

"I don't know how to process the fact that you are only just telling me this story now, Philip. This was trauma."

Philip shrugged. "It was worse for Tony, I think. I mean, I felt guilty about siccing him on the guy, but Tony was never sure how he wanted to wear it—was it something he was proud of, something he was ashamed of? Did he want it to be his reputation, or did he want to get away from it?"

"You were kids."

Philip shrugged again. "Tony still had three months left as a Young Offender when all that went down. Technically."

Annick shook her head. "Ridiculous. A seventeen-year-old boy's brain is as set as the wax in a lava lamp—you're not done developing till twenty-four."

"Anyway, it's all beside the point. Do you understand now why I can't just walk away from the guy because we don't have the same taste in movies or whatever?"

Annick looked in Philip's eyes and saw exhaustion, confusion, pleading, resentment and four beers. She slipped her hand up behind his neck and ear, into his thick, black hair, pulled him over towards her and kissed his forehead.

"Let's go home."

10

OVER THE YEARS, Stephen, a compulsive checker, had missed buses and flights, walked in late on vital business meetings, and blown first romantic impressions by forfeiting dinner reservations to an endless loop of confirmations and reconfirmations which made it nearly impossible for him to ever leave the house. He had been asked politely, if tersely, to find an alternative to his office carpool once it became clear that the tendency to go back incessantly to reconfirm that the front door had been locked was not a passing quirk; having finally found a boyfriend, he had nearly lost him when repeated nighttime trips to the kitchen, to confirm and then reconfirm that the natural gas stove elements were safely turned off—a process that involved his turning them back on, just so that he could shut them off again—continued past the phase in the relationship during which they had seemed cute.

As part of Stephen's therapy, Dr. Boudreau was asking him to slowly increase his tolerance for two related phenomena that no human being, independent of any pathology, ever enjoyed: discomfort and uncertainty.

"And how are you doing with the reassurance-seeking?" she asked, after her patient had laid out his progress, imperfect but in the right direction, since their last session.

"It's okay, I guess," said Stephen, biting his top lip with this bottom teeth. "It's hard. Joey—João—has, like, a harder time than me with it sometimes."

"Not giving you the reassurance?"

"Yeah."

"That's very common."

"Yeah?"

"Totally. With any kind of compulsive or anxious behaviour, anything that causes distress, the tendency with loved ones is to want to do whatever it is in the moment that will alleviate that discomfort, even temporarily. João's natural instinct would be to give you the reassurance that you're looking for, because he cares about you."

"Unless he's working an early flight the next day. Then he wants to strangle me."

"Right. Well, I think we've all brought out some version of that feeling in our partners at some point." Stephen smiled, and nodded. Dr. Boudreau continued, "But reassurance-seeking is just a different way of going back to do the checking compulsion. It's another way of undermining your confidence in your own ability to assess a situation. And ultimately it's another way of placing more importance on the worries, which builds up your sense of uncertainty, and just makes you more likely to check again, or ask again for reassurance. It's that same vicious cycle."

"I know. It's just so hard."

Now it was Dr. Boudreau's turn to smile and nod. This juncture in the conversation was a familiar one, but it never got any easier. There was nothing in the world more natural than bucking against uncertainty, than trying to find assurance in whatever way one could.

"I know, Stephen. But one of the great things about anxiety is that it's not designed to last. If you can sit with the discomfort of not following through with the compulsion, of not asking Joey for reassurance, it won't feel good at first— but it also won't hurt you. I promise you that. And slowly, you'll build back a healthy confidence in your own ability to attain whatever imperfect portion of certainty any of us can lay claim to in this life. Which is typically somewhere south of knowing for sure that there is meaning in the universe, but north of knowing you turned off the stove."

As she was typing up notes from the session in the minutes after Stephen left, Annick heard the phone ringing, confusing her. It rang three times before she realized what it was that had thrown her off: though she was sitting at her desk, it wasn't the office phone next to her computer, but her personal cell, that was chirping.

"Hello?"

"Hi, is that Annick? It's Bonnie Ashford."

"Bonnie? Hi!" Annick grimaced through the uncanny feeling of hearing from someone she liked very much but also wouldn't, under normal circumstances, get a call from. "What's—is everything okay? Sorry, I mean . . . it's great to hear from you, I just—"

"Yeah, it's great to hear from me but it's fucking weird, right?"

Annick laughed. "Yeah, something along those lines. What's up?"

"I just got sort of an odd call from Ivor MacFadden. You know Ivor, right?"

"We've met once, yeah, very briefly. How do you know him? Sorry that's stupid, I guess you would have met over the years through, what—journalism stuff?"

"Oh God, kid, I know Ivor from back when Vancouver was still Vancouver, for Chrissakes. We even—you ever hear that song, that treacly . . . what's it called? 'Uptown Girl'?"

"What, Billy Joel? Yeah, of course."

"Ivor MacFadden and I even lived out our own, more cerebral version of that insipid storyline over, I don't know, say eight weeks one summer back in the late seventies after we met at some university press conference."

"Wow. Bonnie, I never had you pegged as an 'Uptown Girl' type."

"Well, in my defence, our take had a lot more barely sublimated Oedipal and Marxist tension to it. Anyhow, kid, my *shtups* of the disco era, fondly remembered as they may be, are not the reason for my call today."

"I guess not."

"Ivor just called me in the midst of what I can only describe as an *investigation*. The police are convinced that his daughter is a suicide, and Ivor just can't—" Bonnie drew a sharp breath at the other end of the line. "Sweetie, I'm sorry. I know from Ivor that she was your patient. I can't imagine—"

"I—I know. Thank you, Bonnie. It's fine. I mean, it's not—you know what I mean."

"I do. Anyway, Ivor—"

"Wait," Annick said suddenly, wincing, her thoughts catching up to her. "*How* did you know she was my patient?"

"Ivor told me, I just said."

"Yeah, but why would he tell you that? I just meant—that seems strange, doesn't it? Does he know that we know each other?"

"He didn't when he called. But right now you're the only other good guy in his story. You made quite an impression. So your name came up in the telling. When I told him that you and I were friends, I'm not sure who got the bigger bump in esteem, you or me."

Annick closed her eyes and tried to shake the confusion from her head, unsuccessfully. "Bonnie, I'm completely at sea here. What are you talking about?"

"It's very simple, hon. Ivor MacFadden is a man who sees the world in epic dimensions. Has since we were kids. I'd fight with him about leaving a bad tip for a waiter and the next thing I knew he'd be citing Trotsky and talking about Castro and Guevara banning gratuities after the revolution—his world is full of villains and dupes and bloodless bureaucrats and a tiny handful of heroes. Over the past week, he's been neck deep in cops telling him his only daughter is a suicide and a landlord who wants to rent her place to a new tenant and a bunch of her friends who want nothing to do with the wingnut dad she's told them about, and in the midst of all that the firecracker psychologist who tells him his daughter didn't kill herself came on like a white knight."

"I see," Annick said, her shoulders dropping. "I never—I just said that when I last saw her, I had . . . sorry. Never mind. So why did he call you?"

"Ivor was a hell of an investigative reporter in his time. The police think he's the bereaved father of a suicide, mired in denial—but for his part, he figures if they're not going to treat it as much of an open case, he will. He started piecing together that the girl, Danielle, was working for the new mayor. I won't ask you to confirm that, because one, I know you're bound to confidentiality, but two, if that's what Ivor's dug up, I have no doubt that's how it was."

"Bonnie, I still don't understand where you come into this?"

"You remember the Christmas-in-November party? You know: Santa and his rain, dear?"

"Of course."

"You remember what I said about Satan's Hammer?"

"They're pissed at the mayor because he wanted to kill the truck route up from the port?"

"Bingo. Well, that's what Ivor called about. I think he's starting to suspect that Danielle was the collateral damage that helped the mayor change his mind about the route."

"Oh, Bonnie," Annick said, with genuine pain. She felt a heat creep up the back of her neck and a cold grip her chest and stomach. "That's heartbreaking. He's grasping at straws."

"That could be."

"No, Bonnie—Danielle disappeared after Rossi had already announced the decision. The story doesn't even follow. This is not at all a healthy way for him to deal with his grief."

There was a moment's silence from Bonnie's end of the line. "So you do think she killed herself?"

"What?" Annick said. "I don't—Bonnie, this is way beyond my . . . my purview. I'm not competent to speculate on what might have happened to Danielle, but her father's indulging in some sort of elaborate, paranoid fantasy—"

"I can only speak as an investigator, and as a parent."

"Yeah?"

"As for the first? He's not nuts. Aside from the connection he may or may not have to the material, Ivor's not wrong to think that something rotten very likely happened to move Rossi on the Knight Street issue, and the smart money in that event would be on the Hammer."

"Okay, fine, but —"

"As for the second," she continued calmly, "if my kid were taken from me, and there was any way on God's green earth that I could hold onto the idea that he didn't kill himself, sweetie, I'd cling to it until my fingers broke."

Annick let out her breath.

"Bonnie, will you give me Ivor's phone number?"

Annick scrawled the number Bonnie dictated onto the back of a stray envelope; she ripped it off and put it in her pocket, thanking Bonnie, and hung up. Her next patient was due any second now.

✸

Annick grimaced at her canned, iced cashew-milk latte after taking a first sip of what tasted for all the world like an ashtray smoothie. She had impulsively grabbed the drink as a convenient caffeine vehicle while swooping in to the premium grocery store a few blocks from the clinic for a pre-sliced pita, peppers and garlic hummus lunch, packaged and priced for the professional-managerial class. Her plan had been to forgo anything as civilized as a warm takeout lunch in order to use whatever lunchtime she could to get to know Ivor MacFadden.

Ivor's blog was called·*On the Spectrum*—which Annick had to admit, for a politics site maintained by a neurotypical man she'd been told was characterized by ideologically-promiscuous outlooks and an almost reflexive need to piss people off, was a pretty effective name. The site's "About Ivor MacFadden" page was short and sweet; third person in form, first person in content:

Ivor MacFadden is a longtime, award-winning independent journalist without a pension or a party line. Dedicated to democracy, including tradition—Chesterton's "democracy of the dead."

The most recent piece on the blog, posted a few days before Danielle had been reported missing, was titled "The Other White Fragility," and consisted of a nearly two-thousand-word essay on the "moral imbecility" and "unctuous fatuity" of the alternative, white "peace poppy" lapel pins worn by a tiny minority each Remembrance Day, and Annick raised an eyebrow ironically as she remembered Danielle's story about John McCrae's poem. Alongside pieces lambasting the outrages and hypocrisies of cultural and financial elites, which could have been written by any left-wing boomer, there were also a litany of commentaries on "woke" excesses and ritual campus controversy stories, some from Canada but mostly from the United States, and

Annick found herself rolling her eyes both at the content of the stories themselves as well as the vein-popping prose that MacFadden had produced in response.

He felt that climate skeptics weren't getting a fair shake in the media, and wrote glowing tributes to films whose political frames had fallen out of favour (long defences of telling the story of Steve Biko through Kevin Kline, for instance, or paeans to Elia Kazan's McCarthyite heroism); he argued, in a three-part essay series, for the idea that police unions were vital parts of the labour movement.

None of it was anything one could be put on an anti-extremist government watch list for; Annick didn't imagine it was far outside the mean average in terms of a grab bag of views for a white man in his sixties—or any white man. But if you were once somebody's lefty peacenik dad? A former comrade-in-arms fighting nukes and clear-cuts and school closures and scabs? She could imagine it all landing with the effect of an anvil or a grand piano in the old cartoons.

Forgetting for a moment what it tasted like, Annick drew another pull of her cashew-milk latte, and recoiled.

"*Gadelle*, that's disgusting . . ."

"What on earth are you drinking, my dear?" Cedric leaned his long frame against Annick's doorway, pushing his glasses up his nose with a graceful index finger.

"Cedric, you must drink cashew milk, right? That seems very Zen."

"*Cashew* milk?"

"Yeah."

"I'll be damned. I think you've actually found a Buddhist loophole, Annick—suffering without desire."

11

"SOLDIERS WERE DRILLED on these fields during World War One—that's why the park has a cenotaph, in case you're wondering. To a lot of people it seems odd, to have a war memorial smack in the middle of the 'U.S. and Canada Hands Off Everywhere!' district, hacky sack central. But that's why. Young men were prepared here to die on the muddy fields of Europe. There were probably a lot fewer hypodermic needles in the bushes back then."

"Hypodermic needles?" said Annick, rolling her eyes. "Buddy, what year do you think this is? The only thing you're finding in those bushes today are—I don't know. Montessori school pamphlets and labradoodle droppings."

Under the hood of his jacket, Ivor MacFadden gave a mirthless smirk. Surveying Grandview Park from below the umbrella she'd brought in a moment of style-over-substance poor judgment, the only warmth in her body coming from the takeout cappuccino in her hands from Ottoman's Coffee twenty paces behind her, Annick continued:

"If they trained on a day like today, at least the mud wouldn't have come as a surprise."

"No, it wouldn't have."

"You sure you don't want to find somewhere inside to talk?"

"I could actually use the rain and the cold. It's bracing," Ivor answered, staring straight-ahead of himself into the middle distance, before snapping back to attention. "Unless—"

Annick held up a hand to stop him. "I'm fine. I could use the air myself. And I'm not made of sugar."

Ivor nodded, half-smiling again, crookedly, out of one side of his face, the other side incapable of masking his grief and exhaustion. They began walking slowly northward up Commercial Drive towards the mountains, which had to be taken on faith today, hidden as they were behind the grey.

"How are you holding up?" asked Annick, after a few steps. Ivor shook his head, then shrugged.

"When I was a kid, every other movie or TV show was about some kid 'falling in with the wrong crowd'—some June Cleaver mother in a hoop skirt, terrified for her little Biff or Muffin. When we got a little older and too sophisticated by half we used to laugh about it, and now here I am, nearly sixty years old and I've lost my daughter because she fell in with the wrong goddamn crowd."

Ivor stopped talking, in such a way as suggested, to Annick, that he hoped that she would ask him a question. But she wasn't in a hurry. For most people, the silence in a conversation raged like a small, accidental fire—a cloth napkin, carelessly left too close to a tabletop candle, that needed to be swatted down with the same panicked energy, usually with some inane question or air-filling comment. But psychologists—and, for that matter, journalists—had professional experience at not running to let their conversation partners off the hook; not running immediately to puncture the silent tension with a thoughtless application of words and sounds. In a conversation between both a psychologist and a journalist, Annick imagined, the capacity for unrelieved, silent tension could be nearly infinite.

"I thought," Ivor said finally, and Annick felt simultaneously satisfied for outlasting him and angry with herself for turning it into a competition, "that I had raised Danielle with the foundations of a critical, Enlightenment humanism. Those have always been my values, by the way—and when I was a young man that made me some kind of radical liberal and now by some sick magic, in late middle age, it's made me, by the estimations of some of my comrades at least, a reactionary. But Jesus, my daughter was so goddamn bright, and so funny, and to be taken in by a two-bit porkchopping hustler like Alberto Rossi . . ."

Annick noted Ivor's slip into the past tense, in reference to Danielle, and couldn't tell if it was because he no longer thought she was as bright and funny as she had once been, or because he now accepted that she was dead. For the moment, though, that wasn't her primary question.

"Ivor, what is it that makes you think Danielle's disappearance has anything to do with her work for Rossi?"

"Fuckin' streetlamp," said Ivor, then shook his head.

"What?"

"Nothing, strike that. Listen, I happen to think it's not a particularly far-fetched idea. My daughter gets a job as the lone expendable, zero-profile employee of a slimeball pol

84

who goes and picks a fight he has no intention of following through on or winning with the bikers who control the city's waterfront—and now my daughter's gone."

Annick's head bobbled uneasily, hovering between a nod and a shake, and she raised her umbrella at the last second to avoid colliding with another moving southbound on the same sidewalk. The truth was that, on its own, Ivor's theory *did* seem flimsy; but she couldn't bring herself to evaluate it outside the influence of her own theory—itself potentially incorrect, and therefore a distortion—that perhaps Danielle had been Rossi's anonymous paramour; that she had been more than his no-profile employee. Did that have any bearing on Ivor's theory? Make it more or less likely? She still had enough self-awareness to realize that she and Ivor made for a potentially toxic, co-dependent team. Unlike the police, who had brought at least a modicum of objectivity to their investigation, such as it had been, both Ivor and Annick had every reason to cling to, and nurture in each other, the hope that Danielle hadn't killed herself.

The wind picked up now, curling the rain up underneath Annick's umbrella and onto her face. Filling with air, the umbrella lurched behind her shoulders, then threatened to invert before she muttered a string of obscenities, closing it with a damp click and turning up the collar of her black wool coat to the pounding wet cold.

"What kind of Vancouver girl doesn't have a proper raincoat?" shouted Ivor over the rising volume of the weather.

"I'm not!"

"What?"

"I'm not a Vancouver girl! I'm from Halifax!"

Annick dug her hand into her side pocket, to ensure that her phone was still relatively dry. She wondered if she'd be able to find a car share here where they had walked to, or whether she'd have to walk back to Grandview Park. Then it occurred to her that despite the rain, Ivor was pressing on purposefully.

"Where are you going?"

"What's that?"

"I said, '*Where are we going?*'"

"I'm going to the Maritime Labourer's Hall. A Halifax girl like you ought to feel right comfortable there. Maritimer that you are."

"No, I got it. What's at the Maritime Labourer's Hall?"

"Chicken Parm."

"*What?*"

"A fella by the name of Parm Gill."

"Why'd you call him 'Chicken Parm'?"

"It's a nickname. Like calling the seven-foot, three-hundred-pounder at the bar 'Tiny.'"

"But who's Chicken Parm?"

Ivor stopped and spun towards Annick, the rain pounding his hood and beading on his glasses.

"If there's anybody in this city who can offer a hint as to what Satan's Hammer may have done to get Rossi to move on the truck route, it's Parm Gill."

"Chicken Parm?" said Annick, by way of confirmation.

Ivor nodded. "Would you like to come with me?"

Annick didn't answer. She stared into Ivor's face, the rain pricking her cheeks and forehead, and Ivor turned on his heel. Annick chewed at her lip, thinking furiously, as Ivor walked on. She called out: "What did you mean about the streetlamp?"

Ivor turned and smiled ruefully. He took off his glasses, wiping the drops from the lenses with the cuff of his sweater sleeve, briefly looking through them, and replacing them on the bridge of his nose. Finally, he spoke. As soon as he started, Annick remembered the joke.

"A guy's walking down the street one night and sees a drunk on all fours in the light of a streetlamp," Ivor called out through the wet and the cold. "Guy says to the drunk, 'What are you doing?' Drunk says, 'Looking for my keys.' Guy says, 'Oh, you lose 'em over there?'"

"'No...'" finished Annick. "'... but this is the only place with any light.'"

Ivor nodded. "So that's where I'll look."

12

OUTSIDE THE MARITIME Labourer's Hall, two tall men with thick chests and small but very definitely rounded bellies huddled underneath an awning beside a sign reading "No Smoking Within 6 Metres" and pulled unselfconsciously on their cigarettes. Though she almost never caught a whiff of it in her new life, the smell of cigarettes and rain-wetness had been such a staple of Annick's formative years that she recognized the scent before it actually hit her. It was as though she could *see* the smell from across the large, L-shaped parking lot.

The union hall was the anchor of a stubborn block of the old Vancouver at the very northern end of Victoria Drive, in a light-industrial zone that had once, naively, been imagined impermeable to gentrification. For decades, the hot, oppressive stenches of the rendering plant and the factory-farm poultry facility, which could blanket the quarter for whole months of the year, had seemed like some sort of non-negotiable feature of the natural environment, a mountain or a canyon or volcano, that guaranteed against encroachment by the city's dainty or well-heeled. But that was before Vancouver had broken the bounds of economic gravity, leaving all of the old rules behind. In a city without a single lot priced under a million dollars, the town no longer had the luxury of undesirable parts anymore. Craft beer was beginning to seep in around the edges of the neighbourhood, and the long-neglected elementary school a few blocks south received new care and attention now that it was teaching the sons and daughters of film producers and software engineers along with the children living in the Indigenous housing apartments which had always fed it students in the past. But the two men in damp jean jackets, smiling and swearing with gravelly voices and barely dodging the rain, were clear vestiges of the old city, utterly untouched by hot yoga or farmers' markets, and if they noticed Annick or Ivor as they headed into the building, they made no show of having done so.

Parminder Gill was lean and sinewy at about sixty years old, of medium height, with skin a glowing golden brown despite the absolute lack of sun, and a head shaved entirely to the skin except for a silver moustache and goatee which seemed composed of the same number of hairs as might have made up another man's full beard. As Gill rose from behind his desk and came to greet them at the door of his office, Annick felt a short, uncanny pull at the base of her stomach and a fleeting ache twitch across the backs of her thighs. Gill's tight-fitting T-shirt featured a cobra that had faded after a thousand trips through the laundry, underneath the peeling threat that "If Provoked—WE WILL STRIKE," and running lengthwise down the left side of his face, next to eyes as large, round, dark and thick-lashed as a deer's, was a scar that scored his face like a rivulet of sweat. Gill's doe eyes met Annick's; he noticed his being noticed and gave her a gentle, slightly overconfident smile over his goatee which, had she been single, she could have easily imagined lunging for.

"Parminder Gill, International Brotherhood of Long-shoremen; Annick Boudreau, psychiatrist," said Ivor in a sandpaper monotone.

"Psychologist."

"Come on in," Parm Gill said, indicating two chairs across from his desk, in a large office made small by piles of leaflets and newsletters, old picket signs, and framed images of the Indian anti-colonial martyr Bhagat Singh and a young Nelson Mandela in boxing gear. "How long have you known this asshole?"

"Who, Ivor?" Annick asked with a flustered smile. "Oh, he's okay. Then again, I haven't known him for too long, so who knows."

"Word to the wise, whatever you do—don't ever let this guy give you a nickname. They stick like shit on a wool blanket."

"What, 'Chicken Parm'?" asked Annick, turning to Ivor. "That was you?"

Ivor suppressed a smile. "It was a compliment. Like I said, like calling the big guy 'Tiny.'"

"If this is life stuck with a compliment, God save me from ever being insulted."

"Is one of you gonna tell me this frigging story or what?"

"It's your nickname."

"You came up with it. Plus you used to be a journalist."

"Excuse me?"

Gill turned back to Annick, the fun fallen out of his face. "It was nothing, an old showdown from the eighties. Dumb young guy stuff."

"Hardly," said Ivor firmly. "Back in the early eighties, there was a strong bid to organize the farmworkers out in the valley into a union. They were then, as in fact they still are today, among the most exploited and vulnerable and mistreated workers in the province. No bathrooms, children dying in the fields for lack of care, wages straight out of Victor Hugo or Zola, no adjustment for inflation. A significant minority of the workers were actually your people—francophones."

As Ivor said this, Parm looked back to Annick, then down at his desk. Ivor continued, "But the vast majority of them were Punjabi immigrants, against whom there was also, at the time, not coincidentally, a fever pitch local racism." Parm nodded quietly. "I'll point out that the locals in the province, particularly farther into the Interior, didn't much care for your people, either."

"No, that's true," said Parm.

"One weekend, this is back in summer '84, there was a walk-off being staged at Buechner's, a blueberry farm in the valley. Other farmworkers and community members were being driven out to the farm to swell the numbers, and our man here, Parm Gill, all of, what—twenty-two? twenty-three years old at the time?"

Parm smiled indulgently. "Twenty-two."

"Parm's coming up this barely marked, unpaved side access road, driving some borrowed station wagon full of aunties and uncles—I'm talking old men with turbans and grey beards, little old ladies—until he comes upon a pickup parked sideways across the road blocking their path, and three hulking white goons waiting for them."

"Jesus."

"He knows he can't ram them with the car—East Indian guy running over three local good old boys down in farm country isn't going to fly with a jury or a judge, and besides it's going to set the movement back—"

"Holy shit, Ivor, you may have sold out everything you stood for but you're as goddamned long-winded as you've ever been," Parm said. He turned to Annick, half proud, half embarrassed. "I kicked the shit out of them. Please pardon my language. But I got out of the car, and I dealt with the situation, and the old-timers in the car, I guess the word got out and I got a bit of a reputation for not scaring easily. But it's not until a few years later, when I start working in the broader labour movement, that this guy—who you wouldn't know it to look at him today, but was once a good, left-wing journalist—coins 'Chicken Parm' in one of his columns and now it's been more than thirty years and I can't shake it."

"If you think for a second—" Ivor began, lifting his index finger in Parminder's direction, and Annick decided to intervene.

"Ivor, maybe you should just ask what you came to ask."

"Agreed," said Parm, leaning back in his chair.

Ivor looked at Annick, huffing slightly, unsure whether to be grateful for the redirection or to chafe at the interruption. He opted, finally, for the former. "Danielle is missing."

"Jesus Christ, Ivor. Have you called the cops?"

"The cops know. They think she killed herself."

"Holy hell—Ivor, I'm so sorry. And I didn't mean to—"

Ivor held up a hand. "My kid was working for Rossi before she disappeared."

"Who, *Rossi* Rossi? Alberto?"

Ivor nodded. "She was writing the jokes for his campaign speeches. And I want to know if my daughter's going missing has anything to do with Satan's Hammer trying to turn that weasel around on the Knight Street truck route."

Parm leapt up from behind his desk with a speed and grace that gave Annick some insight into how he'd tackled three racist strikebreakers four decades prior. With one hand he slammed shut the door to his office, spinning on the ball of his foot and grabbing Ivor's shoulder with the other hand. When he spoke, it was quietly but with force, through gritted teeth, his face in a guard dog squint.

"Are you out of your mind, asshole? I bring you into my fucking office. You never heard the old saying? What does S, H spell, dipshit? *Sh!*, that's what it spells. Yeah, you smirk all you want, *gora*. You want to set fire to all the good you did in your career, that's your business. You did it a long time ago. But some of us aren't ready to throw it all away just yet."

Ivor slapped Parm's hand away from his shoulder and shuffled to his feet.

"Oh, I don't believe this garbage," said Annick, the contempt in her voice shocking the two men. She might have been especially angry at Parm for having squandered his sex appeal so wantonly, but in any event she wasn't prepared for two men nearing retirement age squaring off in schoolground formation. "You two sit down right this second, for Chrissakes." Both men sat down in their respective chairs, scowling.

"Aren't you the one who's always saying that they don't run the union anyway, that it's a fiction cooked up by the right-wing press to discredit the noble labour movement?" asked Ivor in a belligerent tone.

Parm turned his face up plaintively towards Ivor, pinching the fingers at the ends of both hands. "The papers act like the local is just a wholly owned subsidiary, that the hall is a goddamn bikers' clubhouse. That *is* a slander. Libel, whatever." Parm's voice dropped to something closer to a whisper. "You know I can't vouch that every last man in the local is washtub clean. But I think you know, even in that addled brain of yours, that there's a hell of a lot of good people in the waterfront union, working like goddamn mules out of this very goddamn hall."

Ivor held out his hand in halfway contrition. "Present company included. Especially included."

"But we're grown-ups, right? And certain types of guys, it doesn't take many of them to change the dynamics of a situation. Just because the vast majority of the union is straight and narrow doesn't mean the bad apples aren't a reality. Doesn't mean you can act like a careless goddamn idiot. If I tell you the forest is pretty safe that doesn't mean you go looking for bear caves to piss in."

"I'm not asking you to be a tattle-tale here. None of this is information for a story, or for the police—I am trying to find my daughter."

Ivor's voice had begun, almost imperceptibly, to falter, and Parm's face softened as he thumbed the bridge of his nose. "Ivor, what are you asking me?"

"There is a popular perception that Rossi changed his mind about Knight because someone with a vested interest in the trucking route scared him. I want to know if Danielle is gone because of that."

With his eyes still closed, Parm Gill took a long breath in through his nose; when he opened his eyes back up, he looked first to Annick, then to Ivor. He was halfway seething, half doleful.

"Ivor? As a father—I can't for ten seconds imagine what you're going through right now, where your mind's at. So I get why you're grasping. But this is beyond insanity."

"Did the Satan's—"

"You think they're the only people with an interest in keeping this port alive? There's not a man out of this hall wouldn't have put Rossi's nuts in a vise if he thought it would save that route. I'm talking about the guys who pay their parking tickets now. So if you're asking me, did somebody threaten the new mayor with something scary if he didn't come around on Knight Street? I don't have a goddamn clue. If you're asking me, would I be surprised to know it happened? Not for a second. But to involve a campaign worker? Some young woman writing speeches? Ivor, that's so far out to lunch it won't get back in time for dinner. This is schizoid-grade paranoia. When you started writing that law and order, decline of the West shit a few years back, I was disappointed as hell. Right now I'm just heartbroken."

Both men stared ahead of themselves, at the same spot on Parminder's desk, neither saying anything. Annick turned Gill's words over in her head, agreeing that, if Danielle were nothing more than a part of the communications staff, the idea was crazy. But she wondered if the same held true for a candidate's clandestine lover. If, in fact, that's what Danielle was. Or had been.

"Can you tell me," Ivor croaked, "who from Satan's Hammer might have approached Rossi?"

"You gotta go, brother. Right now." Parm Gill spoke gently, even empathetically, but firmly. "Now. And you can't ever come back."

"I'm not going to—"

"Out." Parm stood.

Annick rose and stepped to the door, placing a hand on Ivor's shoulder in order to give him permission to leave without losing face. Any time she had to neutralize this sort of pissing match with a feminine intervention, it reminded her of growing up, in all the worst ways, and she resented it. But the office was closing in on all of them.

Parm followed them out of his office into the hall, and after a few seconds Annick realized that he was following them out of the building.

"I know where the door is, Chicken," Ivor shot over his shoulder with bleak sarcasm.

"Believe me when I tell you, this is for your own good, Ivor."

After Ivor slammed the exit push bar and stalked into the parking lot, Parm held the door open, first for Annick, then to watch them leave. While they had been inside, the two smokers had been joined by a tall, late-middle-aged white man with shoulder-length white hair and a tobacco-stained white moustache. His blue-and-red mack jacket was open, displaying a black T-shirt with a silkscreen cartoon devil. At the sound of Ivor's dramatic exit, the large man had turned his attention towards the door.

"Gill, you never said there was gonna be strippers," he shouted in a voice that sounded like a jeep being pulleyed out of a gravel ditch. Parm shook his head, while one of the smokers laughed, the other forcing a smile. "What's with all the slammin'?"

"Oh, there was no slamming," said Annick in an attempt at diplomacy, regretting the move instantly.

"The fuck there wasn't, sugar-tits."

"Jesus Christ, Glenn," called Parm.

"What? I didn't say anything. Nobody heard me say anything, did they boys?" The two smokers responded with the same slightly asymmetrical enthusiasm as they had to Glenn's joke. "Who's your friends, Parm?"

"They're leaving."

"Not what I asked, brother."

Annick saw Ivor begin to square off his shoulders and affect a walk something like a rooster's into a cockfight. "Who, me? I'm Ivor MacFadden, won a couple of journalism awards, mounted a couple cabinet ministers' heads on my walls. Would you—"

"And I'm Dr. Boudreau. I'm a psychologist," Annick said before she knew what she was saying, just to cut Ivor off before he started any trouble. "And it's just a really good bra, but thank you, Glenn, you're very charming. Next time try it after wiping the apple juice out of your moustache."

Glenn ignored the remark and jutted his chin towards Ivor. "You doing some kind of little story?"

Ivor gave a joyless smile that bared his top row of teeth, but before he had a chance to respond, Annick interjected, "I'm speaking to local labour leaders about mental health and the union movement. The importance of proper coverage, fighting stigma. Ivor's doing a story on the whole thing."

Glenn licked his lips and stared first at Annick, then over at Parm, then back at Ivor. Finally, he said: "We don't need any fucking analysis."

Annick pulled Ivor by the crook of his arm and they walked away at a brisk pace, diagonally across the parking lot. The one time she permitted herself to look back over her shoulder, Glenn and the laughing smoker had approached Parm and were speaking to him.

When they were out of sight, Annick spun on her heel and jabbed a finger into Ivor's face. He flushed with rage, still keyed up from the confrontation.

"I want you to listen to me very closely," she said. "This isn't the summer after grade nine and you're not nitwit cousin René. I'm not breaking up another pissing match between two dickheads twenty years into prostate exams, do you understand me?"

The prostate line, which had even surprised her coming out, blindsided Ivor entirely and melted the defensive rictus from his face into a peal of laughter. Annick tried not to smile until she knew her demand had been taken seriously, but finally Ivor held a palm outstretched, nodded and said, "I'm sorry." He coughed, looked back in the direction of the labour hall then back out into the driving grey rain and turned finally towards her again. "The night after tomorrow I'm meeting with one of Danielle's comedy friends. Can you join me? I feel like she'll feel more comfortable with a woman there. Plus you can try out your prostate routine."

Annick broke their eye contact and shook her head. "Ivor, I'm feeling very strangely about this. Ethically, I feel like we're getting into a perilous place for me in terms of my practice."

"You were helping her. Now this is helping her."

"It's different. It's not what I'm trained for." Annick struggled to find the appropriate words to say what she really feared, beyond ethical considerations or expertise: that she and Ivor, as the two people in the world with perhaps the most invested in Danielle's not having committed suicide, were merely propping each other up in a mutually comforting delusion. "And I also—I don't know. Never mind."

"What?" Ivor demanded, the rain speckling his glasses with translucent drops both large and small. "What is it?"

"I think Parm may have been right. I—I think, you know, it's possible we may be grasping."

"I don't believe that. And I don't think you believe that."

Annick shrugged. "I'm not sure what I believe."

Ivor nodded. "Well, that's your prerogative. But . . ."

"But what?"

"But she's my baby." Ivor flipped his hood up over his head and turned. She let him leave.

Her hair already soaking wet, Annick opened her umbrella up above her like a comic anticlimax, and began walking eastward, away from him. The tires of passing cars and buses kicked up huge dirty spumes of water that crashed on the sidewalk like surf. A small elderly woman walking a small elderly dog wrapped in some sort of high-performance rain gear passed Annick on her left with an indifference that felt as punishing and grey as the rest of the weather. She tried to walk with energy and purpose, but when the rain was like this it came with a sort of undertow, pulling at the thighs and calves, slowing legs down as in a dream. Both the damp and the chill worked their way right through the wool of Annick's coat, through her sweater and blouse, and she felt the cold clamminess of the city on the edge of winter across the skin of her chest and back. When she was conscious of the muscles in her face, she found them pulled into the tightness of a squinting grimace, a pained exertion. When finally she found herself at the door of the Jerusalem Artichoke, she felt both cheeks release themselves into a smile. She folded her umbrella and went inside.

Her friend Mahmoud was weighted down with two full trays, and could offer only a bright-eyed smile, but his wife, Arwa, stepped out immediately from behind the counter that separated the kitchen from the dining area and threw her arms around Annick. The two women exchanges kisses on both cheeks.

"Oh my God, you are soaking," said Arwa. "I'm going to get you a *dallah* of coffee."

Annick tried to say yes, but felt a trembling in her hands and knew suddenly that if she said anything, she would collapse. Instead, she closed her eyes and nodded.

13

"*SALUT, TRÉSOR.* You want to talk to *Maman*?"

"Oh, well, in that case, sure—please don't let me keep you from whatever is so important that you can't stay on the phone five seconds with your beloved daughter."

Roméo gave a warm and throaty laugh that was enough, on its own, to make Annick smile. "*Non, c'est parce que* Rodney, the kid from across the way, he programmed the TV to tape that barbecue show, and I don't want to miss it. I'm going to make the turkey outside this year. *Un gros dindon de Noël.*"

"That's literally the whole point of taping it, Papa—so that you can watch it whenever you like."

"*Ça mouille toujours?*"

"Twenty-three days straight. No sign of stopping. I'm gathering up two of every animal."

Her father gave the same laugh, only slightly more high-pitched, and she could hear him handing the landline receiver over to her mother.

"*Allô, ma beauté!*"

"*Allô, Mumun.*"

"*Qu'est-ce qui se passe?* Is everything okay?"

Annick turned her face down before lying. "Sure, every-thing is okay." Then, not able to leave it, "Why do you ask?"

"It's in your voice. You fight with Philip?"

"Not really. Maybe a little but it's fine. I'm just—*Maman*, did you ever worry about me? When I was younger?"

"*Ah, oui. La fièvre*—you had a fever, I think you were four years old? For three days straight it's not breaking. Oh, I thought my little one, she's going up with the angels any moment."

"I mean more like . . . like when I was older, did you—did you ever worry that I wouldn't be happy?"

"But you were always a happy girl."

"I guess, but did you ever worry that I wouldn't be?"

"*Non*, why?"

"I don't know. Never mind."

"When your brother is born, you were so excited to be a *grande soeur*. When Claude would cry in the nighttime, when the two of you share a room? Sometime I don't get there fast enough, because you would take him *toi-même* and hold him." Annick gave a bashful smile, as she did whenever this memory was shared. "That's why I'm not surprised even a little when you come and tell me you're going to be a *psy-chologue*. Because from the beginning, anyone is feeling bad, you can make them to feel much better."

The smile went stale on Annick's lips.

✳

Annick's first encounter with bitter melon in Denise Lee's dining room had, by now, grown into the stuff of family lore.

It had been a few months into her time with Philip, after his parents' formal acceptance of their romantic relationship—though his churchgoing folks knew that it was very unlikely that their unmarried son had retained his virginity into his thirties, there had at least been a plausible deniability, and when the invitations to dinner in the Lee family home had begun, it had been seen as a sort of tacit blessing of their ecclesiastically unsanctioned coupling. Annick had consequently felt emboldened to start showing up as the woman known, to some longstanding friends and family members, as Triple-B: Big Brassy Boudreau, the expansive and extroverted Acadian mega-personality who brought fountain-fullness charisma to all social gatherings and every party in need of a life.

When Denise had brought a plate of beef and bitter melon to the table, Annick had disappeared behind a total Triple-B eclipse: "Bitter melon? I don't know who these guys have working in the marketing department, but they need to fire 'em! *Bitter melon*? Don't they know that branding is everything? 'We can't seem to move these bitter melons. Nope, everything else is selling fine, the honeydews, the watermelons, but nothin' doing for the bitter melons or the plums-of-sadness.'"

Philip had giggled, while his parents had simply stared at her, mystified, during the monologue. But after Annick had taken her first bite, Philip's mother had laughed for fifteen minutes straight, and then intermittently for years ever since. Annick had lifted a piece of the meat and the fleshy green fruit to her lips with her chopsticks, and in the first seconds the flavour was utterly unique and absolutely divine; in both taste and texture, maybe the world's most perfect complement to fried beef. Moments later the flavour, though just as unique, became an acrid spread along every surface inside the mouth, and Annick's face had begun to dimple and pinch in the middle like the seams of the steamed dumplings that had constituted the previous course, and if Denise had ever seen anything funnier in her life, Annick presumed that on that occasion she must have required a defibrillator.

But as years progress even the most exotic addition to a family's life grows to be as unremarkable as they are beloved, and the East Coast francophone girl had become a less and less conspicuous part of the Hong Kong immigrant family's West Coast dinners, instinctively serving others before filling her plate, keeping her in-laws' small teacups filled throughout the meal, and even making it through dinner without a glass of milk or water or an after-supper coffee. And tonight, she chewed her beef and bitter melon, having never lost any of her enthusiasm for their thrilling combination, but all of her shock at the fruit's namesake effect.

Annick had also by now made peace with the idea that when she ate dinner at Denise's East Side home, the same Vancouver Special in which Philip had grown up, there was no point at which her hostess would simply sit, relax and eat. In Annick's home, growing up, the very beginnings of meals had been great operatic productions, with each of the meal's elements ferried to the table by an army of siblings and cousins, aunts and, at the helm of it all, her mother; gender analysis of the division of domestic labour had not yet reached the Boudreau household in those benighted times. Great effort was expended in delivering the various components of the supper to the table at roughly commensurate temperatures, with gravies and sauces to round off the uneven patches. But once everyone was sitting, that was it—there was no more work to be done until the plates were cleared, usually by the same people who had brought them. But a meal at Denise Lee's involved a never-ending series of sorties to and from the stove or kitchen counter back out to the dining room, with courses brought as discrete, sovereign blocs within the larger dinnertime configuration. Tonight, Denise had separately brought steamed *gai lan* drizzled with sesame oil and soy sauce, boiled chicken with ginger and mung bean noodles, and now beef and bitter melon with a small tub of steamed white jasmine rice. Having worked in industrial food preparation before retirement, readying airplane meals at a large catering company next to the Vancouver Airport, Denise had never done the work of cooking and serving with great sentimentality. But in the months since her husband, Stanford, had died, Annick noticed that this had begun to change in Denise—since being widowed, after bringing the dishes she had prepared, Denise would now sometimes sit smiling sadly for a few seconds, watching as her son and his lover took their first bites.

"Mom, are you going to eat?" asked Philip. Denise gave a noncommittal wave, accompanied by some vague sound which carried within it the reminder of generational authority, then sat back and smiled as Annick lifted the chopsticks again and again to her mouth.

"None of my nieces or nephews had good appetites when they were small, only Philip. All the aunties and uncles were so jealous for how Philip is eating, even when the other kids are finished and going to play."

Annick smiled at Philip's smile, the way he coolly basked in the praise of his past eating without breaking the rhythm of his current meal. Tucking a mouthful of rice and beef into his cheek, he pointed at his mother's plate.

"Mom, eat!"

"*Ai-yah*," his mother exclaimed, before declaiming a string of sentences in Cantonese that caused Philip to smile, roll his eyes, shake his head and return to his plate.

"Can I get the highlights?" asked Annick.

"It's nothing," Philip said, shaking his head.

"I told him, 'You don't tell your own mother what to do! You want to tell someone what to eat, you have a baby of your own!'"

"Ah," Annick said, returning to her dinner. "Got it."

"I think maybe it's a nice time for you to have a baby now?"

"Mom—"

"I know you both think you have all the time that you like, but it's not true."

"Mom, I think Philip's right . . ."

"And neither do I."

"Jesus, Mom, don't be so morbid."

"Daddy never got to be a *Yeh-Yeh*."

Philip shook his head and said something to his mother in Cantonese that Annick did not ask him to translate. She looked down at her meal.

Denise had filled a small bowl with food and begun to eat, and the three of them sat and chewed in silence for longer than was comfortable. Annick drained the lightly-steeped oolong tea from her small cup, then poured more into those of each of her table mates before refilling her own.

"I feel very strange, lately, about the idea of starting someone else's life."

Denise and Philip looked up at her from their meals simultaneously, each equally curious about dinner's sudden turn for the existential.

"I just . . ." Annick tried but trailed off, shaking her head. The fact is, she wasn't certain what she was trying to say. She thought of Ivor's desperation. Was it for Danielle to be alive? Or was it for her not to be a suicide? Not to have torn up and hurled back that life that her mother and father had given to her?

And what about Annick? She laboured in a world where the idea that suicide was to be stopped at all costs was such a given that the actual, positive value of life was left more or less entirely unexamined. What was it *for*? Could it really be so capricious as to be a joy for some, neutral time-killing for most, and for others, by some Greek myth, accident of biography or idiosyncratic cerebral wiring, just a miserable maximum sentence to be endured from tip to tail? She understood the ethical, even the moral, injunction to save a life already started. But to start a new one, gratuitously, from scratch?

"It's a scary time, for sure," said Philip, shrugging. "But isn't it always?"

"That's not really what I mean, at least I don't think. I mean, it's true, there are so many reasons not to—"

"No," said Denise, waving her hand. She stood up and began clearing dishes. "You don't look for reasons for life. Life is its own reason."

Annick sat for a moment in silence, her mouth full of bitter melon.

"You tell Mom we saw Tony?"

"Which Tony? Tony who?" asked Denise.

Philip looked down at his bowl as he spoke, seeing if he could make the answer sound more casual if he delivered it through a mouthful of his dinner. "Tony Chow."

Denise made a quick, disapproving sucking sound at her front teeth. "*Laan zai.*"

"For Christ's sake, Mom—"

"*Ai-yah!*"

"For crying out loud, how old was Tony the last time you saw him, twenty? People change."

Denise tutted.

"Thanks, honey," Philip said to Annick with depth-charge sarcasm. She twisted her features apologetically and mouthed a silent apology across the table.

"But he's right, Mom. People do change! Look at me—I can't get enough of this bitter melon."

Denise smiled.

✷

A few hours later, Philip located a car-share vehicle a block east of his mother's place, and they kissed Denise while slipping their feet into the still-damp shoes in the front foyer. Philip juggled a repurposed margarine container filled with leftover beef and bitter melon, along with a frostbit ten Tupperware container of ox-tongue stew—"the meal that kisses you back," according to Big Brassy Boudreau—and so Annick hoisted the umbrella up for both of them like a torch.

The night was cold and damp, but the darkness was cradling, and life felt much smaller around them, cozier and somehow more manageable. As the car came into view, Philip forced a bleak laugh.

"I'm sorry about the baby stuff."

Annick shrugged forgivingly. "She wants to be a grandmother."

"She does. And she knows I want to be a father."

Annick turned to Philip and smiled as softly as she could; she leaned and nibbled gently at his ear. "I know, *mon coeur*."

Philip waved his fob over the car's front dash, unlocking it for both of them. As he started the engine the windows fogged to an instant opacity, and they sat listening to the tinkling classical piano playing on the public radio station preferred by the vehicle's previous driver. As the interiors of the windows cleared, the exteriors blurred from rain, and Philip snapped the windshield wipers into service before pulling out into the single-lane side street, crawling slowly through the wet darkness.

"We couldn't stay in the condo," said Annick as though no time had passed since the last beats of their dialogue, and Philip made a sour face.

"First of all, that's not true. At least not to start."

"It's a one-bedroom, *cher*."

"Oh, suddenly it's a one-bedroom," Philip said, smiling now. "This whole time it's been a one-bedroom-plus-den."

"Fine," Annick said, laughing. "But a kid can't live in a den. Especially not a Vancouver den. Especially not a Coal Harbour den. Christ, a goldfish couldn't live in our den."

"It would be more than ample for the first couple years. And afterwards . . . we'd have more room."

"Oh we would, would we? Are we annexing the neighbour's solarium?"

"No, I just—what I'm saying is, if we wanted it, we could have more space. Even a yard."

"I'm not moving to the sticks just for a yard, *mon amour*. I'm not trying to be a snob. I just don't like Frisbee enough for the commute."

"I'm not talking about the suburbs."

"Well maybe you could stop talking in cryptograms so that I might have some idea what you *are* talking about."

"Why do you think my mom is still in the house?"

Annick spun in her seat. "Woah, wait—*what*?"

"She's holding onto it for us. For when we have a family. It wouldn't be a gift exactly, I mean—we'd still have to line up a place for her, a little condo or something on the East Side—"

"Boy I can't tell you how much I love finding out my life is being planned in my absence, Philip. I can't tell you because words don't go down that low."

"Would you calm down? Nobody's planning anything. We had one conversation—"

"And when were you going to tell me about it?"

"I'm telling you right now!"

"Philip, I love our place. I'm not in any rush—"

"Dude, would you get off my ass already?!"

"Um . . . *pardon-the-fuck me*? First of all, did you just call me 'dude'?"

"No, sorry. This guy behind us is riding right on my frigging bumper." Philip stared with quiet menace into the rearview mirror, and Annick turned again in her seat to look behind her. As she did, the car flooded with high-beam light, and she shielded her eyes with her hand.

"What a dink," said Philip.

"We're dinks too, unless I let you blow it," Annick said, turning back around in her seat as Philip turned onto Nanaimo Street.

"Huh?"

"Double income, no kids." Philip smiled and shook his head.

Annick turned the volume up on the piano music against the growing intensity of the rain on the car's roof and windows as they moved north down the broad, empty street before turning left onto Hastings.

"It's Glenn Gould," Philip said softly, and for a second Annick softened in the aftermath of their argument, marvelling at her Renaissance Man, her handsome ex–tough guy turned science journalist who could identify a Glenn Gould recording by ear, until she looked at the radio panel in the middle of the vehicle's console and realized that the digital light-up screen identified the recording as it played on the radio. That was twice this week that she had overcredited his sensory powers. She covered her mouth to conceal a fugitive burst of telltale laughter, not wanting to tip Philip to the wholly undeserved amnesty he'd nearly finagled, when from behind the steering wheel he spoke again.

"He's still behind me." Philip was narrowing his eyes once more into the glare of the rearview mirror. Annick turned again to look and again, on cue, the car filled with the light of high beams thrown by the car behind them. The car's engine growled as it advanced on them, closing the distance between the two vehicles.

"What's going on?" asked Annick, knowing even as she did that Philip had no reason for knowing the answer.

"I have no idea who it is. Some asshole kids? I think they're driving a Charger—do you know anyone who drives a Charger?"

"I take it that in this context a Charger is some kind of car?"

As she spoke, the vehicle behind them jerked into the empty oncoming lane, roaring past them, and then yanked itself back in front of them so suddenly that Philip had to slam on his brakes. Stopped maybe six inches behind the Charger, they sat motionless in the middle of Hastings Street, the rain pounding on the roof of the vehicle, the other driver revving the muscle car's engine and Annick reaching out a finger to extinguish the Glenn Gould concert.

Philip threw the tiny two-seater into reverse, spinning the car backwards; the Charger mimicked the movement in reverse, pulling a U-turn, too bulky to catch up when its driver realized that Philip was in fact executing a full circle. As Philip and Annick hurled westward, the growling Charger first lumbered and then sped after them, getting always bigger in the rearview mirror.

"Howe," Annick said.

"How what?"

"Pull up Howe."

Philip hung a left into a stale yellow light at Howe, and swore under his breath as the Charger took the same turn, screeching through a hard red.

"The Jacobean Court. Take it to the valet."

"What are you talking about?"

"Into the hotel, the valet!" Annick screamed, pointing Philip into the driveway of the hotel, an upscale, exclusive set of downtown boutique accommodations and ballrooms. "It's crawling with bellhops and cabbies and all sorts of people. Witnesses."

Philip pulled into the driveway of the Jacobean Court, drawing the heavily logoed car-share Smart car up behind a silver Bentley to the evident disgust of the handsome young parking attendant in red jacket and black bow tie.

Annick and Philip sat in the car, their hearts pounding in their ears and necks, watching the rearview mirror. As though the reflection couldn't be trusted, Annick turned her body around once more to look and saw that the Charger had stopped its pursuit. Only as her breathing began to slow could Annick hear the valet, his palm out, his voice muffled by Philip's closed window, asking for the keys. Still panting, but with her heartbeat beginning to slow, she reached a trembling hand into her purse and pulled out four twenty-dollar bills. She opened her door, walked around to the driver's side of the car and gave the money to the attendant, now drunk with bewildered gratitude.

"Just give us a second sweetie, okay?"

"Yeah, sure," said the boy dutifully, bounding back to his station as Philip emerged from his seat.

"What the hell was that?" Philip asked, stupefied. "You think that was the other shoe finally dropping? With Mike? Lewis Blair?"

Annick shook her head. Ever since she had helped to imprison the nephew of a local and well-connected businessman and nightclub owner, Lewis Blair, she and Philip had been half-awaiting a possible fallout of some kind. But Blair had had ample time and any number of opportunities to avenge his family and his loss of face. This, tonight, had felt urgent and intense.

"What do you want to do now?" Philip asked.

"Maybe we should go in for a drink, just to buy some time?"

"Okay."

Philip gave the keys to the valet, explaining that they wouldn't be long, and as he held the door of the hotel open for Annick, her phone began to ring. It was Ivor MacFadden. As they made their way up the lobby stairs, she answered.

"Hello? Ivor?"

When he spoke, Ivor's voice sounded slurred and dampened. The muscles tightened in Annick's chest, and the skin of her back and shoulders slickened with a sheen of cold sweat.

"Ivor? What did you say? Where are you?"

"I'm in the emergency room," he said, with enormous effort. "VGH."

"What happened? Are you okay?"

"They got me."

14

AFTER HER YEARS at McGill, years spent on the mid-century subway trains and sex-drunk streets of Montréal, Annick had always laughed at Vancouver's big city pretensions—having grown up, herself, in a medium-sized, coastal, provincial port city, she had immediately seen the family resemblance despite the straining efforts at sophistication in her new home. But when she had returned to Halifax to tend to her father at the depths of his illness, the heights of his cancer's aggressive and expansionist ambitions, the crumbling structures of the Victorian hospital where he lay had left her reeling, and she had since developed a kind of stupefied admiration for Vancouver General. The complex near the middle of the city was more like a small neighbourhood, a few large, venerable buildings anchoring the facilities, providing the hospital's continuity with the past, while all around them smaller, newer, more architecturally daring efforts paid tribute to advances in medical care and to the magnanimous capitalists footing the bills for construction with some of the money left over after not having to pay taxes. Just across from the emergency room sat a medium-height building with the look of a crystal decanter, named for David and Helen Truscott. Annick wondered briefly, as they passed it, whether those might be Miles Truscott's parents, or grandparents. The emergency room was named in no one's honour.

Annick asked for directions at the triage desk, and afterwards she and Philip made their way through the inhuman fluorescent glare and all-too-human groaning of the ER's various chambers—the large open waiting areas which fed into each other creating, over the course of hours, the illusion of forward momentum. Ultimately they came to a large room whose sundry miseries were vivisected by as many blue curtains on rails, enclosing each of the patients who were lucky enough to have made it to a bed and miserable enough to need one, and protecting them from everything but the hospital's sounds, smells and invisible microbial agents. An exhausted nurse pointed Annick towards one such curtain, closed three-quarters of the way, at the far end of the room, and her anxious dread hung so thick in the air around her that, as in a nightmare, the faster she walked towards it, the farther away it seemed.

Her first thought, as she pushed the curtain aside and saw Ivor where he lay, was that he was dead. Annick felt the call for a nurse, a panicked cry for help, rise up out of her chest and she just barely caught it before it left her lips. She stopped when she noticed the tiny rising and falling of the thin hospital blanket over his stomach. Otherwise, Ivor no longer looked like the man she had seen the day before— *the* man, or *any* man; in fact, he only barely looked human. Under his eyes spread large raised purple welts, and a blackened gauze bandage ran from the top of his forehead down his left temple to the area in front of his ear. Another bandage, this one red and jellied, was stuck to his chin, and three of the fingers of his right hand, along with two of those on his left, were taped into metal splints. Ivor MacFadden and Roméo Boudreau were very different men in some respects, but each was a tough and charismatic father, vibrant behind his moustache and under his silver and whitening hair—and each man likewise shrank to helpless, childlike dimensions against the canvas of a hospital bed.

"Jesus," said Philip over Annick's shoulder.

"Let's go. He can't talk. I'll come back tomorrow." Annick closed the curtain as quietly as she could, trying not to rattle the metal rings, and turned to find Philip's hand outstretched.

"Come on, let's get home. It's been a night, man."

"Danielle?" The name had been moaned from behind the curtain. Philip jutted his head back in the direction of Ivor's bed, and for reasons she couldn't quite understand, Annick took almost the same care with the metal rings as she opened the area back up.

"Ivor? It's me, it's Annick. I got your message. But we don't have to talk now, sweetie. I can come back in a little while."

"And she's gonna be okay?"

"Ivor?"

Ivor sat slightly forward, as though he were only now actually waking up, then let himself drop gently back down against the inclined head of his bed. "Annick. You got my message. I—thank you. Who's this?"

"Ivor this is my boyfriend, Philip." Philip gave a silent, masculine nod from behind her, and Ivor tried to set his features in such a way as to show his approval for the gesture, with mixed results.

"You got a good girl, here," he said, bobbing his head as he said it and folding in his lips, and Philip smiled and nodded again to cover over the clumsiness of the exchange.

"Ivor, we're going to let you sleep, okay? We can talk about what happened later. But we don't have to leave. I'll stay just outside here. Is there anything you need? Philip can grab it." Philip nodded a third time.

Ivor grimaced and shook his head. "No, no," he said, frowning. "I'm fine, just a little groggy from the painkillers. Plus I'm not supposed to sleep for long anyway," he added. "Concussion." He had seemed to want to punctuate this last word by jerking his thumb up towards his head, but managed only a claw-like open-palmed lift.

"Oh my God, Ivor. I don't even know what to say—this is just awful."

"*Bull*shit."

"What?"

"I just got shellacked by a couple of Hammerheads, told me nobody's interested in reading about traffic. What does that tell you?"

"That you have a concussion?"

"Christ, I thought you were sharper than this. They so much as admitted they put the scare in Rossi! That spineless, Chamberlain slug—I'll have his goddamn Adam's apple for sauce."

"So *that's* who was—" Philip began, but Annick cut him off with a hand gesture not subtle enough to evade Ivor's notice.

"What?" he asked. "That's who was what?"

"It's nothing," Annick said calmly.

"*Bull*shit," replied Ivor.

"Annick and I just got chased down Hastings Street by a mystery car," Philip interjected, "and from what I gather, these were the same guys, or the same type of guys, as put you in here? Ivor, there's no chance you're just a civilian unbound by doctor-patient confidentiality who can tell me what the hell is going on here, is there?"

Ivor looked at Annick. "You haven't told him?"

Annick turned her palms towards the ceiling and shook her head. "He's usually a very good psychologist's spouse. In all our years together, this is the first time I've ever seen him grasp for a loophole."

"Loophole," said Philip with mock contempt, rolling his smiling eyes. "I just pulled a *Dukes of Hazzard* through the Downtown Eastside and I'm not even allowed to know why!"

"Your lady friend is my daughter's doctor. My daughter— she's been having a tough time lately, although . . . there's not much I can say about it in detail, because I haven't been a part of her life for several years now. She was working for Mayor Rossi during the campaign, writing jokes—my daughter's a comedian. She was born one. But she's gone."

"I'm so sorry," said Philip. "I mean, did she—?"

Ivor shrugged as best he could. "She's disappeared. The cops think it's suicide because she's on antidepressants, and they found a note, a suicide note. No date on it, though. But Annick says she didn't kill herself—"

"Hang on—Ivor, Philip, I'm not at all comfortable with—"

"—and I say she didn't kill herself, because something about Rossi's U-turn on the truck route reeks of bikers, and just a day after we get made at the waterfront hall asking impertinent questions, they lay a beating on me and they chase the two of you through—" Ivor's sentence cut off in a hiss of air as his face folded in on itself, tightening into a knot of pain as he lurched forward in his bed and grabbed at his side.

"Ivor!" Annick exclaimed, gently taking hold of his shoulder. She turned back to Philip. "Phil, can you go get a nurse?"

"Of course," he said, disappearing into the room, whose beeping and talking and crying momentarily came back onto the plane of Annick's consciousness before dissolving again as she turned back to Ivor who was sitting forward now, staring down at nothing in particular.

"I'm fine. He doesn't need to get a nurse."

"Of course he does. What was that?"

"They broke my ribs."

"*Seigneur . . .*"

Ivor's eyes seemed to be going in and out of focus, and Annick was inclined to credit the concussion until he spoke again, and she realized that the distance in his look was more meditative, more melancholy.

"Did she suffer, my little girl?" he asked, turning his broken face up towards Annick. Ivor's leaky eyes were watering, and he fought a quiver in his bottom lip. She didn't know what to say.

"She was always funny, right from the very beginning," he continued. "She would sit and watch old comedy sketches with me—I had a half dozen tapes, old VHS tapes, of SCTV . . . I'd play her Monty Python records. I'm talking, she's a little,

little kid, and she's just squealing with laughter, so she'd get the hiccups. My wife would get so mad at me, but I couldn't help myself. There was no sound like that in the world, nothing on earth like the sight of her little teeth, her whole face smiling. These days, they send you to the Hague for telling some of the kinds of jokes we laughed at then—these miserable Puritan times with our sanctimonious nihilists." He shook his head, first at them, then at himself. "Writing that kind of sentence is what pushed her away from me, I guess."

"It's complicated," Annick offered, and Ivor was in the mood to accept it.

"Did she hate life?" he asked her, his eyes filling now with walls of water in front of their uncanny, concussed pupils. "Did my little baby hate life?"

"Ivor, she's my patient. I know you love her, and I know you're worried about her. But she still has a right to her privacy."

"I'm her next of kin," he answered, a warble in his voice.

"Hey, Ivor. Right now, you and I are the only two people on the planet treating this thing like 'next of kin' doesn't come into it, okay? Danielle's privacy rights are a going concern. Don't crap out on me."

He squeezed the tears out of his eyes, then nodded.

"The guy's coming in a sec," said Philip as he returned to Ivor's bedside.

"I don't need a nurse," Ivor began tersely before catching himself. "But thank you."

"Is there anything you do need?" asked Annick.

He nodded. "As a matter of fact, yes."

"Name it," said Philip.

"I won't be in any shape tomorrow night to talk to that comedian. Hell I don't even know if they'll have let me out by then. I need you to go and talk to her."

"Oh, Ivor—I can't do that!"

"Why not?"

"For starters, because it's your meeting! And I'm Danielle's doctor. And I don't know what to ask, and I—"

"You're her doctor," Ivor interrupted. "That's fine, it's good, I know I can turn to you to care for her well-being. But this isn't about that. I was meeting with this young lady to see if I could get some more details about how she got connected with the campaign, maybe see if she could put me in touch with her contact in Rossi's camp. Get a feel for Danielle's place in that world, that kind of thing. Now I can't do it, Annick, so I'm begging you. Christ it's got nothing to do with her treatment, nothing to do with your work with her. All it's got to do with is this rotten fish situation at City Hall, and at the port, that's put me in hospital, put you two in a car chase and maybe swallowed up my little girl. Please?"

Annick pounded the heel of her foot against the hospital floor, and ran her palm nervously now with, now against, now with the grain of her pixie cut. She looked first at Philip, then at Ivor.

"I never should have touched that frigging curtain."

✳

When faced with high-stress or anxiety-provoking circumstances, Philip's only two responses were either intense physical exertion or else a nearly comatose kind of sleep, and given that the lateness of the hour when they finally reached the condo meant that the gym downstairs was no longer accessible, he passed out widthwise across the bottom of the bed within a few minutes of getting home. With Annick, though, stress landed differently, and she knew that the evening's nightmares meant that she wouldn't be asleep until the hours were small.

On the couch in her pyjama pants and one of Philip's CBC T-shirts, Annick used the tiny remote control that she was otherwise always losing to peck through more YouTube videos, this time of Alberto Rossi.

Most of the videos were of Rossi the candidate: a keynote speech at the Italian-Canadian Federation of British Columbia; a sunny summertime charity walk against spinal meningitis; there was a stunt video in which he stood on the deck of Miles Truscott's stately blue motor yacht moored at the Granville Island market and got his friend to commit to supporting a pledge to link moorage fees to fuel efficiency at all Vancouver marinas. Cleverly, Annick thought, Rossi never appeared to run from what might strike some as an unseemly coziness with one of the city's blue-blooded developers. Instead, he played up the fact that his best friend was among the especially rarefied fortunate who might feel the brunt of his policy experiments most sharply, and that this camaraderie proved mutual good faith.

"I lost a debate tournament to a young Alberto Rossi way back in grade twelve," Truscott announced in a low and steady voice, to polite laughter from the journalists gathered around his vessel. "And I was a smart kid—I promised myself right then and there it would be the last time I'd ever be on the wrong side of this guy." The video ended shortly after a gregarious Rossi clapped his hand on Truscott's shoulder, then leaned in for a masculine half-hug.

In every one of the videos, it was easy to see both what had initially repelled Danielle about Rossi as well as what might ultimately have attracted her to him. He was over-polished, tended towards unctuousness and was so evidently taken with himself that he was unable to escape the pull of his own gravity.

But he was a beautiful man—dark, deep Mediterranean features and thick, soft silver curls; not tall, but lean-stomached and broad-shouldered, with thick biceps and perfectly shaped hands decorated with a broad gold wedding band and a loose-hanging gold bracelet. His teeth were impeccable under an always-confident smile.

The next video thrown up by the algorithm featured Luciana Rossi and Tavleen Dosanjh, his campaign manager turned City Hall lieutenant. Posted by an account called The Vancouver Society, the video was titled "vs Presents: Women in the City—an Evening with Luciana Rossi (Rossi Consulting/Advocacy) & Tavleen Dosanjh." The clip was forty-five minutes long and had been viewed just shy of eleven thousand times.

In it, the two very elegant, well-dressed and intelligent women, separated by about twenty-five years and just a few feet, sat across from each other in overly large, too-soft grey chairs, of which they both occupied only the very edge. They conversed into their respective microphones, held on perfectly aimed tripod boom stands, cheated out towards the audience at just the slightest angle so that the dialogue felt both genuine as well as performed.

They spoke about childcare in community centres, night-time safety on and around public transit, and gender parity across traditionally male-dominated areas of city hiring and contracting. They talked about shifting the municipal tax burden from businesses to property owners in a civic economy so dominated by inflated land values. They talked about the importance of representation, and of a range of women role models, and at this point the conversation digressed into a relatively tasteful and controlled mutual appreciation.

Dosanjh clearly admired the older woman, but Annick couldn't get a read on Rossi. There were no self-deprecations or false humilities, but there was a vague edge, a sense of uneasiness that Annick couldn't quite pin down, in the way she interacted with her husband's staffer.

If Rossi had been sleeping with Danielle—had that been the first time he'd strayed? And whether it was or wasn't, did Luciana know, or suspect, that her very handsome and self-regarding husband wasn't to be trusted with his young staffers?

Could these two women, each capable of a forensic analysis of municipal issues with great nuance, subtlety and empathy, also be capable of something as petty, albeit human, as fighting over Alberto Rossi?

If so, could either of them have hurt Danielle?

Annick felt an aching, exhausted sadness seeping into each of her limbs, but the thought of sleep, with its certainty of bleak and restless dreams, disquieted her. She entered "Danielle MacFadden stand-up" into the search bar once again.

There was nothing there she hadn't already seen.

15

"MY PARENTS GREW UP in the Philippines, and my dad is super Catholic. I didn't actually know how Catholic he was until we were about twenty minutes into what I thought was a conversation about atheism, and I realized that he was just talking about Protestants. Like I was like, 'You know, from an epistemological standpoint, it's interesting that materialist naturalism presumes a reductionism that is itself not a naturally given hermeneutic.' And he was like, 'Yes, and they don't pray to Mary.'"

Django's had been a Cambie Street fixture for decades, a Vancouver outlier in that it had held on to its look, feel and purpose through various iterations of ownership and evolutions of taste. In the days before the city had reinvented itself as a polyglot foodie paradise, Django's had been serving plates of tapas drizzled in olive oil to customers seated cabaret style around a massive wooden stage, upon which women with long, brown ponytails danced flamenco to the music played by male guitarists with ponytails of the same length. When Annick had first moved to the city, before meeting Philip, a dead-end date with a handsome but otherwise uninteresting high-school social studies teacher, which wouldn't have led to anything on its own steam, received an assist from the flamenco and culminated with a return to his apartment. When she had left, a few hours later, it was with the distinct feeling that it hadn't been as good as the dancing. Even now she could remember the movement of the dancer's hips under her long red dress; the look on the guitarist's face as though he were crying rather than singing; the relentless stamping, again and again, of the dancer's shoes reverberating against the wood of the stage. That anything so staccato could also be so sexy had been, to Annick, a revelation.

At the other end of the spectrum of human sensuality, Django's had also been the site of a long-running, amateur-leaning stand-up comedy night, where new and aspiring comics could try their hands at humanity's least-forgiving creative form shy of the trapeze in a largely supportive atmosphere. The massive bullfighting posters on the wall offered subtle reminders of what the stakes normally might be in the world of stand-up comedy, where chances were always best that someone would get gored. But the Django's audience understood that, like someone getting their hair cut by a student barber, they should adjust their expectations. Towards the end of the show, after the beginners, a handful of professional, working comics—women and men with TV credits, comedy albums and years in the trade worked into the confidence of their posture, their premises and their punchlines—would come onstage and try new stuff, or prepare for bigger, more important shows in front of bigger, more important audiences.

It was Daphne Rosario's show for the time being— she booked it, she hosted it and she returned to the stage between each act, righting the atmosphere whenever a bomb had gone off, keeping things moving at a brisk pace if someone had done well and things were sizzling. Daphne was plump and handsome, with large glasses taking up most of a winsome face, and she smiled readily without punctuating her own material with the kind of onanistic laughter in which a number of the other young comics indulged. Annick watched Daphne from a seat at the bar. She was good: funny, charming, comfortable in her own skin—but there was still something ineffable that separated her performance from Danielle's; some ill-defined border between dedicated and even talented amateur and consummate professional. It could have been Daphne's four-dollar words and professorial gait as she paced the front of the stage. She was a smart person being funny, rather than a funny person being smart— could it be as simple, or as stupid, as that? Annick looked down at the now-emptied Irish coffee in the saucer in front of her, running her finger along the inside of the cup to collect the last bit of creamy foam that had collected around its edges, and wondered if instead, spooked by the possibility of having lost a patient to suicide, she was now romanticizing her, retrospectively inflating her qualities in a way unfair to the living and breathing Daphne. She wondered if she was now looking at Danielle through Ivor's eyes.

Annick had arrived too late to introduce herself to Daphne before the show, so she had instead taken her perch at the end of the bar, ordered her hard coffee and taken in the performances like any of the other two dozen or so audience members scattered throughout the room. The evening's comedic offerings, uneven though they were, had been a welcome distraction from the vise-grip anxieties of the previous days, including an argument with Philip, just after they'd finished speaking to the police about the incident on Hastings Street, over whether or not it was safe for her to go to the show alone. Philip tended to be sparing with his outbursts of chivalry, and on the whole Annick found them to be more harmlessly charming than anything else, but something about his insistence on protecting her tonight had been grating—maybe it was the fact that she had to acknowledge that there was, indeed, potentially some danger still in the offing. But she couldn't abide a lover who was also a babysitter, and she was finally able to make the case that leaving the condo on her own in a Lyft might in fact be the least conspicuous way to travel.

She asked the bartender, a tall man in late middle age with Scandinavian features, for another Irish coffee and he gave her a solemn nod from out of a Bergman film, totally incongruous with the laughter bubbling around them as one of the promised professional comedians took to the stage. A short, thin, silver-haired woman in aviator-style prescription glasses was holding court, and Annick knew instantly that she had not fantasized the difference between a gifted hobbyist and an inspired professional.

"I'm a mother, and so I—kid, are you seriously fucking texting right now? That's how little time you have for a female perspective in comedy?" An embarrassed young man in a baseball cap, sitting in the front row, put his phone down apologetically, his cheeks flushing. "Or did you just hear the word 'mother' and think, 'That reminds me, I should be sullenly staring into an electronic device right now.'"

Annick laughed as the rest of the audience hooted its approval for the young man's ritual humiliation, and the giggling offender himself buried his face in his hands.

"Always staring into a phone, two inches away from the screen. At least when I was your age and boys went blind, there was ejaculate involved," the comic continued, to an applause break, as the Max von Sydow bartender laid Annick's drink down in front of her. She lifted the mug to her lips and felt the cool whipped cream under her nose as she sipped the scalding coffee, its burnt-bitter roast rippled by the grassy alcoholic strength of the whiskey, and for a moment the cold, wet dark of the Vancouver fall was powerless over her.

"I had my kids before anybody told me that we weren't doing that anymore in Vancouver. We don't really do that in this town anymore, unless you're like a billionaire war criminal or something. It's tough to raise two kids in a studio-plus-solarium." Annick smiled and thought of Philip, then stared for a second at her drink, the smile faltering for a moment on her face. "No, Vancouver has been zoned for one-way vaginas. My girlfriend told me I have to move the family out to the suburbs. She moved to Coquitlam and she keeps trying to get all of us to move out there with her. My other friend thinks she's just trying to get us to share in the misery. But I think she's trying to re-found Vancouver thirty kilometres east. My friend lives on a street called Sprucewood Crescent and her kids go to a school called Pine Tree Elementary. Everything is named like that out there—which will save you a lot of heartache because trees almost never turn out to have been racist."

✳

Annick lingered at the bar after the show let out, watching the comedians politicking nervously in their corner, some seemingly trying out jokes on each other that they hadn't had the nerve to try onstage, others withdrawing into an uneasy quiet. Particularly compelling to Annick—who had studied the intricacies of anxious behaviour and knew expertly the subtle patterns left by the fight-or-flight instinct across a whole range of human behaviours—was to watch people who had laid themselves bare in front of a crowd of strangers, telling stories most others would take with them to the grave, but who could now, in the intimacy of one-on-one conversations, not maintain eye contact. She was fond of telling her patients that everyone was a chemistry set, emphasizing that there really was no inner limit to the individuality and idiosyncrasy of every individual, but moments like these drove the point home even for her.

After paying for her drinks, Annick slowly began to orbit Daphne, just close enough to signal that she was there to speak with her, keeping just enough distance not to be pulled into a conversation that might involve anyone else. However, the silver-haired headliner—now wearing an adorable hot-pink raincoat—departed the comedians' corner, making a point of noticing Annick with a smile as she waited.

"You were so funny," said Annick.

"Thank you," said the comic, her magnetism undimmed offstage. "And you were so good-looking."

"Ouch."

"What, no good?"

"Do you hit on everybody with the past tense?"

"Listen, your past may have been tense but our future is bright."

Annick felt her cheeks warm. "I'm afraid it's the perfect continuous conditional for us—spoken for. Flattered, very. But spoken for."

The comic allowed herself a half-hungry look and then gave a subtle smile. "I would've loved to bring you home and introduce you to my grammar."

Annick turned, still smiling, to look over her shoulder as the headliner walked out into the rain, feeling the trill of the flirtation in each of her extremities, among the first uncomplicated and unalloyed feelings of pleasure and contentment that she'd had in days. Her idyll was interrupted by a voice from behind her.

"You looking for a spot?"

Annick turned back to find Daphne's face, solicitous and uncynical, smiling at her wide-eyed.

"No, sorry, I—great show."

"Aw, thanks! We try."

"I was—my name is Annick, I'm a friend of Ivor, Danielle's dad?" At this, Daphne's face became instantly solemn.

"Oh right—yeah he texted me that you were coming. Is he okay? What happened?"

"Yeah, he's—" Annick began, before remembering that Ivor was not, in fact, fine, despite her autopilot answer. "Could we maybe sit for a second? Someplace just a little bit more private?"

"Yeah, of course."

Daphne nodded goodnights to a few straggling comedians, pointing loosely to Annick in wordless explanation for her exit from the scene. The two women sat at a small, round table in a corner, and Daphne briefly furrowed her brow, jutted her bottom lip and smiled.

"From what Danielle has told me, I didn't think Ivor had any friends who weren't angry old white men."

"Well, I haven't really known him that long. Give it some time and maybe he'll sour on me. Or I'll turn into an angry old white man."

"I guess I shouldn't be laughing—he said there's something wrong with Danielle? Is she okay?"

"I can't really—that's what we're trying to sort out."

Daphne shook her head sadly. "Oh, Danny. She talks about this onstage, so it's okay for me to tell you—she's had a really tough time lately. Depression. She even started putting aside some money every month to see a psychologist." Annick tried to continue nodding unselfconsciously. "I hope she's okay. The thing is, I thought she had really turned a corner the last few months, ever since she started working on the campaign."

"You got her that job, right? I mean, Ivor mentioned that you had connected her with the Rossi people."

Daphne nodded. "Danny and Tav and I were all at SFU at the same time together, but they didn't know each other. I knew both of them though."

"And Tav is . . ."

"Tavleen Dosanjh. She was president of the student society when we went there, so I mean, Danny knew *of* her, but she didn't *know* her. Tav's always been political, tons of drive. She's his left hand, now."

"Sorry?"

"Rossi. Sorry, I'm in pretty deep on this stuff, all the civic politics Twitter feeds and even a couple of podcasts. I literally could not be less cool if I tried," she smiled. "But my dissertation is a comparison of South Asian and Southeast-Asian representation in Vancouver electoral politics at all three levels of government. Poli-sci. Which is another reason why Tav and I have stayed in such close touch. Anyway, the joke is Tav's the mayor's left hand, Kingsley Davis is his right hand, Miles Truscott is his brain and Luciana Rossi is his super-ego. The only parts of Alberto Rossi that are Rossi's are his ass, his face and his dick."

"Wow," Annick said, her eyes widening.

"Sorry," Daphne laughed.

"No, it's good to know. So Tavleen came to you because Rossi needed a joke-writer?"

She nodded. "That's right. Rossi was super wooden and he was pure social media cringe, and so Tav was looking for somebody funny and politically literate that the campaign could bring on."

"And you didn't want the job?"

Daphne affected a mock *tsk* and feigned a slap on Annick's hand. "Girl, look at you being all sweet!" She laughed, then indicated the interior of Django's with a wave of her hand. "No, this is my comedy world. I have no pretensions, I'm good here. One day when I'm a miserable adjunct in some rural university no one has ever heard of

I'll have my memories. Besides, it felt a little too close to my research area. And I knew Danielle was perfect for it, even if she didn't."

"She didn't want the job?"

"Not at first, no. She thought Rossi was a sellout, and a neoliberal. Kind of an empty suit. Which, fair enough. But I knew she'd be great and that she needed a steady paycheque for a while." Annick immediately buried the thought that Danielle might have needed the job to pay for her therapy. "And I thought she would hit it off with Tav, which they did, at least to start with. Tav and Danny are opposites in a lot of ways, but also really similar. They're both so gorgeous, and they've both got that intense charisma that just totally draws people in. Honestly I think part of me was just interested in seeing what would happen from putting the two of them in the same room. I didn't know things were going to go so sideways between them."

"What do you mean?"

"We never really got into it—I think because each of them knew how much I cared about the other. But they both stopped having anything nice to say about the other after a little while. It actually got really icy."

"And you don't have any indication as to why?"

Daphne raised her shoulders. "Nope. I mean Danielle had, like, the opposite experience from what she was expecting in that whole world. All the people she expected to hate, she started to really like—after a while you couldn't get her to say a bad word about Rossi, even joking. But she also really liked Truscott, said he was decent despite his money. I mean, she hated Kingsley, which she expected, but anyone who'd even so much as caught his picture in a newspaper would've seen that coming. And I think things really soured with her and Tavleen."

"I see. What about the others on the campaign?"

"I don't know—what do you mean?"

"Did Danielle get along with them? Did she ever have any problems with Luciana Rossi, for instance?"

"Um, not that I know of. I mean, from what Tav tells me, Mrs. Rossi is a little weird around younger women."

"How so?"

"Just, like—it's very important for her that she's seen to be holding the ladder down behind her, but she doesn't want anybody climbing up it, you know?"

"I think so."

"I just always got the sense from Tav that Luciana Rossi was one of those women who preferred working with men."

"I don't want to put you in an awkward position, Daphne, but do you have contact information for Tavleen that you could share with me?"

Daphne first grimaced, then raised her eyebrows over a look of resignation. "You know what, I'm not sure I would really feel comfortable anyway, to be honest—but these days having Tav's phone or email is barely any different from not having them. She's so busy, I don't think I've heard back from her since the election."

"I understand. That completely makes sense."

"You could always try crashing one of the Four Five Six Summits," Daphne said, smiling.

"The what?" Annick first thought that Daphne was rolling her eyes at her, before realizing that she was rolling them at herself.

"Sorry, I really do read *way* too much of this crap. The 'Four-Five-Six Summits' is the local media's extraordinarily obnoxious name for the daily morning meetings between Tav and Kingsley before the mayor's day starts. Bit of colour in the power-behind-the-throne profile pieces. At *six* in the morning, *five* days a week, they meet in a café kitty corner to City Hall for *four* shots of espresso each and plan out his worship's day."

"My God that's psychotic. And I love espressos. What's the café called?"

"Bean Through the City."

"And here I thought the 'Four-Five-Six Summit' was the worst thing I was going to hear tonight."

"Oh honey, it can always get worse."

Annick thanked Daphne and ordered a car on her phone, waiting inside, as she had promised Philip she would, until it arrived. She sent him a text:

J'arrive mon coeur. xo

A few seconds later, he responded.

All good tonight? No problems?

She tapped back.

Only for you. Hit on by a highly
talented lady. I have options.

She smiled as she watched the ellipses in his text bubble, waiting for his reply.

worse comes to worst you guys'll need
a pool boy on the compound. we can
talk all abt it tonight. very slowly

She shook her head.

Can't. EXTREMELY early morning tomorrow.

16

ANNICK HAD LEFT Django's with the vague and very unscientific hope that the whiskey with which her two coffees had been rendered Irish might act as a countervailing force to the caffeine that they contained. But little besides some sort of powerful pharmaceutical sleep aide could offset the effects of two moderately sized cups of fully caffeinated coffee after nine p.m.—and even if alcohol tended, for her, to bring quick sleep, it also brought poor sleep. There were, in short, likely no two poorer choices of drink ahead of a pre-dawn ambush than a pair of Irish coffees. Of course, by late November, in this city, "pre-dawn" could refer to any part of the day before about eleven a.m. But by five thirty-five in the morning, with two hours of fitful sleep to sustain her, Annick was hunched puffy-eyed in the corner of Bean Through the City over a six-shot cappuccino that she had ordered—first against the barista's recommendations, then virtually against his will. From her reflection off the shiny back of the large espresso machine, Annick did not imagine that she would be encountering any flirtations this morning.

Somehow, the café looked exactly like every other coffee shop built any time in the last ten years, with the same combination of cream, chrome and shiny sand-coloured lumber in precisely the same proportions as could be found in any other sterilely cool yet vulnerably earnest competitor anywhere in the city. As she'd watched the young white man with a grey toque and light moustache design a semi-abstract floral pattern into the foam of her monstrous request with quiet competence, she'd listened to the plaintive and vaguely aristocratic music playing quietly on the shop's speakers from what she assumed must be his phone, and had been partway into speculating on the nature of his master's thesis—say, *Problematizing the Heteronormative Anti-Colonial in Frantz Fanon* or *Discursive Realms of Online Belonging: Interrogating the Instagram Direct Message*—before deciding that she was only being a bitch because she'd had two hours of sleep. At her seat, she took a sip of her coffee, which tasted, as he'd insisted it would, like a frothed book of spent matches, and she regretted the lack of respect she'd shown for a man who knew his trade. She reached into her wallet for a five-dollar bill, slipped up to the front counter and dropped it surreptitiously into the tip jar.

As she spun on her heel to return to her seat, the front door of the café opened and Kingsley Davis, wearing a smart grey knee-length jacket, beaded with rain, over a Burberry scarf whose ends were fed through a prep school loop around his neck, entered tapping a black umbrella against the side of his leather boot.

"Hey Mischa," he said in a calmly resounding voice, to a wan wave from the man in the toque. "Can we get round one?" Mischa nodded his assent coolly. As Kingsley sat to lock immediately into some apparently pressing task on his phone, Annick was given the immediate impression that his convivial attempts at making himself into a beloved regular were being met with icy if passive resistance. She truly had judged the barista too hastily; she was beginning not only to respect but also to admire him.

Three minutes later, when Tavleen Dosanjh entered, there was none of the down-home-regular act; she walked briskly, instead, directly to Davis's table.

"Hey. You order?"

"Yup," Kingsley answered, before looking up from his phone. "Mischa's got round one on the way."

"Cool." She removed her jacket and hung it on the back of the seat. She was as beautiful as Daphne had said she was, looking even at this hour just as glamorous as she had at the Women in the City panel, with large features and a head of miraculously thick raven-black hair pulled into a loose but elegant bun. If an onlooker didn't know that these two were the mayor's top lieutenants, they would have guessed that they were some kind of power couple on the rise.

For all of its breathless local media branding, however, the Four-Five-Six Summit seemed an underwhelming affair, at least to start with. Listless Mischa brought out two double espressos in demitasses and saucers, to a perfunctory nod from Tavleen and oleaginously over-performed good buddy gratitude from Kingsley as the two mayoral aides pecked independently at the phones in their hands. After their first sips, a low mumbling began across the table, and after a few minutes, Kingsley stood and sauntered towards the till, ordering the second round of double espressos and paying for all four. Annick wondered idly if they alternated paying for the coffee or whether this was all part of a two-front offensive by Kingsley against both Mischa's affective resistance and the expenses deduction line on his Canada Revenue Agency filings.

Annick didn't know when the right moment was to make her entrance—she could only see a long string of possible bad moments—and so as Davis and Dosanjh began their second cups, Annick collected whatever bearings she still had about her and walked over to the table.

"Pardon me, I'm so sorry to bother you—but may I sit for a moment?"

"No," Tavleen answered flatly.

Kingsley was predictably more solicitous, but to the same ends. "I'm sorry, this is actually a work meeting."

"Yeah, this is about your work."

"Excuse me?" asked Tavleen, though the words were also written across Kingsley's face, which had very quickly shed its warm skin.

"I need to speak with the two of you about Danielle. Danielle MacFadden."

"Who are you?" asked Kingsley, allowing the subtle beginnings of a squint to creep into the corners of his eyes.

"I'd like to sit down, please, and explain."

"My friend said no."

Annick's body quickly ran itself through a series of physiological threat-responses, which she had rehearsed ten thousand times with panic and anxiety patients over the years. She felt the sweat stand out on her palms and back; felt the muscles tighten across her chest; felt a dizziness and an uncoupling from reality—she knew each feeling clinically, its full Darwinian backstory, but none of that made it feel any more pleasant. She opened her mouth, so dry now that it felt and tasted like a pile of old newspapers, and spoke very quietly, in as flatly threatening a voice as she could, understanding that there was no turning back from what she was about to say.

"Danielle's father, who is a journalist, was hospitalized the night before last. He was beaten by members of the Satan's Hammer Motorcycle Club after he asked at the waterfront who it was that got your boss to change his mind about Knight Street. If, for whatever reason, you can't find the time to speak to me this morning—"

"Sit down." It was Tavleen who spoke. Kingsley was still staring at her with his mouth open.

"Thank you," Annick said, trying not to tremble as she pulled out her seat.

As she sat, Kingsley snarled defensively, but at a volume controlled to keep his Bean Through the City charm offensive unbesmirched. "First of all, and I'll say this to anyone, anywhere, eight days a goddamn week, leaving that trucking route in place was the right policy, full-stop."

"It wasn't the policy your candidate ran on," Annick said from in the depths of her exhaustion. It wasn't necessary for her to fight the principle of the policy decision or the ethics that had lain behind it, and she silently cursed herself for engaging.

"Campaigns are complicated. You're juggling hundreds if not thousands of stakeholders in a dynamic situation that's constantly shifting."

"Yes, I understand what dynamic means."

At this, Davis snuffed like a bull, red creeping up the sides of his neck. Annick regretted her snark, and inwardly berated herself for letting her exhaustion get the better of her. "I'm sorry, I don't mean to be rude."

"No, you're just blackmailing your way into conversations at six in the fucking morning, Miss goddamn Manners."

"Who are you?" asked Tavleen, but her partner was on a tear.

"You ask anybody in this town which is the bigger threat to civic life, hyper-gentrification and property speculation or some particulate matter in the air along Knight Street and nine and three-quarters out of ten will say it's no contest. The point-two-five out of ten are asthmatics who live on Knight Street."

"Kingsley," Tavleen said, showing her impatience now.

"So you expect me to believe that the mayor did a one-eighty on his own policy just because he decided it was the right thing to do for working-class Vancouver? All six families left?" Annick bit her tongue, literally, to make up for not having done it figuratively.

"Why not?!" Kingsley shot back, scandalized. "Rossi was an East Van candidate, full support of labour, history in the labour movement—"

"And a best friend who's also a piggy bank!" She decided that it wasn't her morning for restraint.

"Who, Miles? That's not fair. In fact, you're arguing against your own case—if Miles called the shots, Knight would have been practically closed to vehicular traffic and turned into a fully serviced pedestrian boulevard for a string of gated communities, for Chrissakes. This has got shit all to do with bikers. It's the right policy. Even that woke priest says so."

"What priest?"

"What's her name, the Jamaican one."

"She's Bahamian," Tavleen said icily. "She's the priest at St. Clare's, just off Knight in the thirties."

"It's a woman priest?" asked Annick, still tired and confused.

"Jesus, what is this, a riddle about who can operate on the little boy?" said Tavleen. "It's an Anglican church."

Annick pinched the bridge of her nose. "I'm sorry—I'm Acadian, I've had two hours of sleep, I was raised Catholic, you said St. Clare —"

"Anyway the *point*," said Kingsley, "is this Reverend what is it, Carmichael, has been one of the squeakiest wheels in the city about getting the truck route shut down. Mostly environmental stuff, but even she just came out, posted a sermon saying that if the thing wasn't being drawn down in an organized way, it was just going to be a gold rush land grab, make the rich even richer and make this city even harder to stay in." Davis sat back in his seat, satisfied, the smug calm having crept back into his face.

"But you didn't want to talk about the truck route," guessed Tavleen.

"Not directly, no."

"What do you want to know about Danielle?"

"Are you—did you know that she has disappeared?"

Dosanjh nodded. "The police contacted the mayor's office, obviously. We told them what we knew. It's very sad. Suicide is tragic."

Annick tried to run calculations in her head, but thoughts kept getting lost in the fog of exhaustion. She tried to go over what it was that she knew about Danielle from their sessions, the privacy of which was sacrosanct, and what she knew from the search into which she'd been drawn—into which she'd allowed herself to be implicated—by Ivor, and by her own hopes. She braced herself, and pounced.

"Did you turn on Danielle because her affair with Rossi ended one that you were having with him?"

The look of seething contempt on Tavleen's face was so strong, immediate and visceral, that Annick knew right away that she had landed impossibly wide of the mark. As Davis's face slackened into one of little boy terror, Dosanjh's snarled with offended dignity, her top lip undulating softly, almost but not quite baring her teeth as she spoke.

"Don't you fucking dare. Do you know how long I've been awake? This morning? More than an hour. And before this morning I've been up for more than twenty years. While you were cutting your Barbie's hair I was sitting at my dad's feet at the woodworkers' local. I was staying up with my grandfather to hear Indian election results and British election results. And every goddamn day I went into that campaign trying to do everything I could to beat the men who hide behind the tall hedges on the other side of town. So when I gave Danielle a chance to help us, and he couldn't keep his dick out from under his feet—"

"Tav—" Kingsley tried.

"—yeah, they *both* let me down. They *both* embarrassed me. But we were in it, so I swallowed it. And we won. I won. And the second we did, I told him that if he wanted me on staff, he had to act like a grown-up. He had to end it." Now she furrowed her eyebrows, and Annick watched as two small tears began streaming down Tavleen's face. "I'm sorry she couldn't handle that. I'm sorry she killed herself. I didn't want for her to kill herself. But it's not my fault. It's not my fault."

"Tavleen," said Kingsley, with less kindness.

"I didn't kill her," she said, and when Annick reached out to soothe her, she threw up her hands and walked out.

17

SUNLIGHT WAS STILL the stuff of urban legend, and Annick made no effort to shield herself from the cold rain as she plodded the few blocks from the café to the West Coast CBT Clinic, staggered with guilt for what she'd said to Tavleen, with grief for Danielle and finally, for the first time in days, with sober, clear-sighted despair.

Not only could she see, now, what had been so obvious to Tavleen—that her depressive patient, buoyed temporarily by an energizing love affair and plunged just as quickly back into despondency by its ending had, indeed, committed suicide—but she felt the weight of her therapeutic failure, not only in the lead up to the tragedy, but also in its aftermath.

The wet sidewalks were sleek but not shining, and Annick slipped and nearly fell in the impassive, snuffing morning darkness. She thought of the six patients that she would see that day—Gerry, 51, general anxiety; Aisha, 23, OCD; Dennis, 31, OCD; Winston, 28, panic disorder; Tatiana, 21, OCD; Deborah, 44, PTSD—and of how useless she would be on the fumes of her sleep, with her concentration inevitably splintered. Each of them deserved the same degree of care and attentiveness as Danielle had—more; they were still alive, still reachable—and yet she wouldn't be able to provide it today. She cursed herself, and how short she came up against the memories of her mentor.

Dr. Conte had wrestled martyrdom from them in the midst of a hot June seminar, the Montréal air nearly as humid as the atmosphere she trudged through this morning, only heated to baking, binding shirts and skin and soaking every hairline in the classroom. Annick imagined, in retrospect, that Dr. Conte had deliberately chosen an oppressive day for the instruction—that the mortification had served a pedagogical purpose.

"*Martyrdom*," she had said from the front of the seminar room, stretching the three syllables across the full width of her Italian accent with a derision she otherwise almost never evinced, "is a three-fold failure of the practitioner, betraying *doctor, patient* and *practice*." Maintaining a sweep of collective eye contact, Dr. Conte had punctuated the weight-bearing terms mid-air with a triumvirate of thumb, index and middle finger, pecking the ideas into their heads. "I want you to imagine, for a moment, a *field medic* in the Great War. Having treated a young, injured soldier, let us say from the farmlands that fed the city where the doctor grew up, he becomes sympathetically identified with the soldier's woundedness, his injury, and becomes committed to ensuring his safety at all costs. To this point, his commitment is commendable. But if we press it? At what point does it become *pathological*?

"Let us imagine now that the doctor discovers that the barely recovered soldier is to be part of an offensive on the enemy's line which will take him up and over the trenches? Senseless, yes. Unfair. But now, mad with concern for the safety of his patient, at the injustice of his being sent, still wounded, into battle, the doctor runs out ahead of him into no-man's-land to shield the farm boy from the enemy's bullets. And what is the *result*? Dead doctor. The soldier, still dead. And his remaining comrades, each one just as fragile as he was, left in the mud without a medic."

Annick unlocked the door to the clinic, illuminating the space in stages with the slow, perfunctory flipping of several switches, and silencing the shrill of the alarm system with the tap of a code she was honestly surprised to have remembered. This was, by her count, the second time in the entirety of her professional life in which she had arrived ahead of her colleague Cedric, who she imagined might not be there for yet another hour. In the small office kitchen, she emptied a damp, cold coffee filter filled with spent ground beans into the countertop compost, wincing against the smell as she opened it, but taking no joy in the aroma of the fresh beans she set to percolating in their place. She stomped in pure, dazed inertia to her own office, the machine grunting and bubbling behind her.

Depression was different. It wasn't just that so much of what she treated at the clinic, so much of what she saw patients for, session after session, was anxiety disorders, whereas depression was a mood disorder—though there was that. Over the course of a day, Annick could see patients for obsessive-compulsive disorder, generalized anxiety, panic attacks, agoraphobia or post-traumatic stress and feel as though she was moving from table to table at a large family reunion; some distant cousins, yes, but also siblings, even some twins; recognizable features cropping up in wildly different contexts, lit up by entirely different lights but still familiar.

Most importantly, though, she could tell them, in an honest and uncomplicated way, that their anxieties were *irrational*, or, at the very least, expressing in an irrational way. She knew with utter certainty that the patient whose body and mind were screaming that they were still in the house fire that killed their siblings was not, in fact, still in that fire; she knew with something analogous to mathematical precision that the new mother obsessed by the terror that she would involuntarily molest her infant child was no threat to anyone; she could explain empirically why staying in the living room until the end of one's life was the incorrect mode of navigating the inevitable threats and uncertainties of existence.

But what about depression? It was different from nihilism in principle, sure—but did the distinction hold around the edges? She could look with clinical eyes at weight gain or weight loss, at the disappearance of libido, the inability either to sleep or to wake up, the avoidance of friends, family, work and play. She could isolate behaviours which, if indulged, would immiserate depression; she could identify the reflexive negative thoughts that could fuel it. She could recommend a course of modest activities to build up competencies and confidences: there was exercise, mood monitoring, ways of challenging and changing thought patterns, journal-keeping.

But could she tell them, with anything like clinical certainty, that life was worth living?

For thousands of years, philosophy in every corner of the globe had been shadowed by the irrepressible thought, sometimes expanded and elaborated by the most luminary minds in human history, that existence was pure nightmare; a tragic absurdity defined by meaningless suffering. On good days, it didn't seem that way—but could she really answer the charge in a satisfactory way? Dr. Boudreau could confidently assure a patient that they didn't have to wash their hands seventy times in one day; but could she tell a patient, with the same assurance, that tomorrow was worth being there for, whatever the struggle? Or was that just a point of view?

⚹

Annick jerked forward in her chair.

"I tried to let you sleep for as long as I could," a mellifluous voice inflected by notes of Jamaican antecedent and Zen calm intoned from her doorway. "But the workday is about to begin in earnest."

"Cedric," said Annick, rubbing her eyes with her fingers. "Thank you."

Cedric walked softly across the small office, laying one hand gently on her shoulder and, with the other, placing a large cup of coffee with precisely the right amount of milk in front of her on her desk. She smiled up at him warmly, and he turned on his heels for the hallway.

Annick sipped at the coffee as she turned on her computer and waited for it to boot up. She looked out the window, noticing that the rain had become a mist against the glass. She retrieved a bottle of mouthwash from the bottom drawer of her desk and crossed the corridor into the office's shared washroom.

After scooping a few handfuls of water first into her mouth and then onto her face, Annick gargled and spat, and as she did so, ran her conversation with Tavleen Dosanjh and Kingsley Davis over again in her head. She stared into the mirror.

Returning to her office, she googled "is st clare a saint for anglicans," and discovered that, at least according to Wikipedia, St. Clare of Assisi is venerated by Roman Catholics, Lutherans and, indeed, throughout the Anglican Communion. She searched for St. Clare's Vancouver, and though the small Anglican parish did not have its own website, it did have a Facebook page, upon which a user named RevBeatrice Carmichael, accompanied by a small thumbnail image of a smiling, late-middle-aged Black woman in glasses and clerical vestments, had recently written the following post:

Dear siblings in Christ—there has been a great deal of confusion and disappointment about recent developments in our city and in our parish with regard to the Knight Street trucking route. Many of you have asked for the text of my recent statement on the matter at Parish Council, which I'm now sharing here:

One of the early heresies rooted out by the Patristic Church was that of Marcionism, which held, among other things, that Christians were bound only by the New Testament scriptures and not by the Hebrew Bible or so-called 'Old Testament.' Here and now in the 21st century, I still encounter a great deal of what I like to call 'Marcionism Lite'—the desire to skip over the messy, difficult parts of our scriptural heritage to get to the stuff we all feel good about. In the New Testament there is no distinction between Greek or Jew, whereas the older books are full of tribal warfare, ugly conflict, of nations warring for land and resources. Easy to choose which one we'd rather identify with, no? And yet, if we're honest, which set of circumstances is more like the world in which we live today? We live in a city, a province and a country built on stolen land—land which our church helped to steal. Throughout it, we, the colonial first-person plural, identified ourselves with ancient Israel. Marked out for great things by God. But the prophets of ancient Israel were always a fiery and inconvenient reminder that the nation had been marked out, too, for special responsibilities by God—to the orphan and the widow, the alien, stranger and neighbour. The children of this parish of St Clare's deserve clean air to breathe and safe streets to cross, as they and future generations of children deserve safe levels of carbon in the atmosphere. Our care for these children, the air they breathe and the atmosphere that cradles them are each part of our stewardship of Creation. They deserve it, just as much as we all deserve to live in a world without distinction between Greek or Jew. But we live in the messy world of a stolen city, and we can't get to things out of order. In our campaign to phase out the Knight Street truck route, we have insisted from the beginning on a careful and deliberate drawing down, with supports from every level of government, and engagement with the Musqueam, Squamish and Tsleil-Waututh Nations, to ensure that the Knight Street left in its wake is a safe, more vibrant, more inclusive neighbourhood. An overnight decommissioning, which would have amounted to a hand-out to the city's richest developers, would have been utterly self-defeating. I close with another piece of wisdom from the Hebrew Bible: there is a time for every matter under Heaven.

Annick sat back and took another sip of her coffee. She scrolled up and read the next post from RevBeatrice Carmichael: Evensong 5:30 p.m.

She googled "evensong."

18

FOR ANNICK, entering an Anglican church felt something like going into a restaurant that had closed in its original location and moved to a new one with two-thirds of the same stuff; a few of the same paintings and wall ornaments were still there, but now at slightly different heights and distances from each other; there were new menu cards but with most of the same choices. The handful of times she'd been inside bona fide Protestant churches—visits to the Chinese-Lutheran parish where Philip had been baptized and his father eulogized, for instance, or the marriage in the United Church of Trevor and Matthew, two formerly local psychologists who had wed before leaving to start matrimonial life and a new practice together in Victoria—everything was different enough from the Roman Catholic parishes of her childhood that they felt legitimately like something new. The dearth of liturgical pomp, the subdued if not downright austere aesthetic of the services, made them almost entirely their own thing, a separate species under the Christian genus. But it felt as if the Anglicans got partway into the Reformation and then got distracted; it was still all candles and mystical sacraments, and rather than the difference between, say, French and Italian, the difference between the services felt more like that between Spanish and Portuguese. The resemblances were such that Annick had to remind herself that the sight of a woman at the altar in a clerical collar marked, on its own, a fairly big departure.

The Acadians had never undergone the same dramatic, politically charged and, historically speaking, nearly instantaneous secularization as their Québécois cousins, and so the presence of the Roman Catholic church in Annick's life growing up had been taken for granted, which cut both ways; it had been wandered into without much thought, and wandered out of with the same. She'd never had any defined break with her Catholic upbringing, beyond the fact that when she'd moved to Montréal for school, she acceded naturally into the absolute and unexamined secularism of life in contemporary Québec, where the bright white cross which lit up on Mont Royal was more like the black-and-white photo of a long-dead ancestor than the convincing show of ecclesiastical force it had once been. She didn't have anything in particular against religion, besides the knock-on effects that it could have on some of her patients, particularly those with OCD. Besides the relatively common problem of intrusive, unwanted blasphemous thoughts in spiritually devoted OCD patients, there was the difficulty of disentangling the concept of prayer from the pathological idea that thoughts alone could project effects into the physical world. Cognitive behavioural therapy, like the immense majority of successful evidence-based therapeutic treatments, proceeded on the assumptions of scientific reductionism.

Judging by the turnout for Evensong, so too did the immense majority of Vancouverites. Aside from Annick, there were three other people in the congregation: an almost impossibly elderly woman; a dark-haired man of about thirty with eyes of devastated sadness; and a smiling fat man of about sixty, wearing a black shirt and clerical collar and a pair of brown corduroy pants. If Reverend Carmichael was disappointed with the turnout, she showed no signs of it, smiling warmly at the assembled, locking into eye contact with each of them, before extending her hands, palms upward.

"Welcome to Evensong at St. Clare's, thank you so much for being here with us tonight. In this time and place we are gathered on the ancestral and unceded territories of the Musqueam, Squamish and Tsleil-Waututh Nations. Light and Peace in Jesus Christ our Lord."

"Thanks be to God," replied all but Annick in easy and organic unison, and so she added her small echo after the fact, earning another gentle smile from the priest.

Evensong consisted of the reverend delivering a sort of plaintive, melancholic chanting, the eerie and delicate beauty of which was punctuated by her short readings of scripture as well as collective recitations of the Creed and the Lord's Prayer from the assembled in the same simple chant. After her territorial acknowledgement, the priest had turned sideways and delivered the liturgy in profile. There had been handouts at the front of the church with all the text necessary to participate in the service, but after the first five minutes, Annick had laid the paper down in her lap, letting the unadorned music of Carmichael's alto voice wash over her like an incoming tide. The missing sleep of the previous night tugged around the edges of her eyes and mind, but something about the scene held her in place, and after about twenty minutes, it was all over.

The elderly woman went and clasped Carmichael's hand in hers for a moment, and the youngish man with the sad eyes crossed himself and knelt, mouthing the words of a silent prayer as the older man dressed in clerical-casual style attended with jolly efficiency to the extinguishing of candles. Once more, as she had on comedy night, Annick found herself hovering, though it didn't take long for the priest to make her way over to where she was sitting.

"Hello, welcome."

"Thank you. You have a very beautiful voice."

"Oh, aren't you sweet—thank you, my dear. I'm Beatrice."

"Annick."

"I'm sorry?" the priest responded, and Annick thought she detected a slight alarm in her eyes as she did.

"Um, Annick?"

Carmichael's face broke into a warm smile. "I'm sorry, *Ah-neek*. That's lovely. It's French?"

"By way of Acadia, yeah."

The priest now allowed herself a soft laugh. "I thought you meant you were from ANIC, and I thought—well, okay, let's build bridges!"

Annick shook her head, dumbfounded. "I'm so sorry, I don't follow at all."

Carmichael waved a hand dismissively. "Very inside baseball. The Anglican Network in Canada—ANIC. Split from the Anglican church in 2005. The guys who think we've just become a bunch of postmodern liberal Pride paraders.

Twitter with a little bit of Jesus." She gave a self-deprecating smile. "Are you new to the church?"

Annick shook her head, then nodded. "No, I mean—I'm not Anglican, I'm not really . . . I mean I grew up Catholic, I was baptized and confirmed and all that, but I don't really—I feel very rude saying this here, and I don't mean this at all disrespectfully," Carmichael shook her head sympathetically. "But I don't, myself—I don't believe in God."

Carmichael was a listener, and she nodded receptively and understandingly, her open face inviting further trust and disclosure, and Annick had the dizzying feeling of sitting in the patient's chair.

"I'm sorry," Annick added nervously.

"Are you apologizing to me, or to . . ." the priest indicated heavenward theatrically with her eyebrows, and both women laughed. "I'm just glad that you came this evening, and I hope that you'll always feel welcome to join us here, whatever the shape of your going metaphysical framework."

"I had actually—" Annick began, but trailed off.

"Yes?"

"I'm not sure why I came. God, I'm so tired. I think I came because I wanted to talk to you about your post, about the Knight Street truck route."

"Oh, okay. Certainly."

"But I'm not even sure exactly what it was I wanted to ask. Are we—" Annick looked around the church to confirm that, by now, the other worshippers had departed. "This may be a stupid question, but if I'm not a member of the church, are you still bound by—like, is this confidential?"

"I consider confidentiality, within the usual ethical caveats, to be a sacred element of human trust and communication. I find that to be true in both a pastoral context and otherwise."

Annick squeezed her eyes closed for a moment gratefully. "I have—I guess you'd call him a friend, who was hospitalized. He was beaten up. By men from Satan's Hammer—" Annick giggled nervously. "Sorry, it just occurred to me that they're literally called Satan's Hammer."

The priest shrugged. "Some bad guys are less subtle than others. I am very sorry, though, to hear about your friend."

"He was looking for his daughter, who is missing. She's disappeared. She's probably—the police, everyone thinks she's killed herself. They're probably right."

"Oh," exhaled Carmichael softly but sharply, as if in genuine physical pain.

"But she worked for the new mayor and he, my friend, he thought that maybe her disappearing was bound up in the business around the truck route. In the threats, maybe, that the bikers might have made against the mayor—if they made them. And it sounds ridiculous to me even as I say it, only the second we started asking around about the mayor at the waterfront, my friend gets put in the emergency room, and my boyfriend and I nearly got run off the road . . ."

"Sweet Jesus . . ."

". . . very deliberately. And I have since confirmed that his daughter, and he doesn't even know this yet, but—that she was much closer to Rossi than just being a member of his staff."

"But would these people have known that?"

It was a sharp and thoughtful question, and it put Annick on the back foot. "I'm not sure. I guess I don't know." If Annick, as Danielle's psychologist, hadn't even known about the affair, did it make sense to operate as though the city's biker gangs did?

"You've gone to the police?"

"Sort of—I mean my friend's assault was obviously reported, and we called in about the chase down Hastings Street. A cop came by our place and took a statement. But to them, the bits and pieces we've been able to pick out, they don't amount to much. And they really only take any shape around a disappearance that they don't find all that mysterious to begin with—for them, his daughter is technically a missing person, but they know she had a history of depression, they found a suicide note —"

"There was a suicide note."

"Yes, but undated. This was someone who has struggled with major depressive episodes for a long time—that note could have been written any time in the past two years, at least."

"Did you tell this to the police?"

"I gave them my clinical opinion."

"Your, sorry?"

Annick looked down at her hands. "I was—she's my patient."

"I see."

"There are people within the Vancouver Police Department who don't much like me, because of how things went with a previous patient of mine who was wrongly arrested, nearly railroaded for murder."

The priest raised her eyebrows. "You are . . . some doctor, I would say."

Annick shook her head. "Do you think it's possible—I mean, would they be bold enough to threaten the mayor? Have they ever threatened you for your activism?"

"No, but the mayor and I are two very different beasts. I'm an immigrant in a clerical collar, some woman as far as they're concerned. It's very likely that the motorcycle enthusiasts made the altogether correct inference that I failed to rise to the level of a threat worth dealing with. In the scriptures, a voice in the wilderness gets his head on a plate—these days, they've figured out that for the most part, a voice in the wilderness is like a tree falling in the woods. But Rossi's another matter entirely. He could have killed the truck route."

"I mean, that's what he said he was going to do."

"Sure—in the election, it burnishes his green credentials and wins him favour with the developers, besides keeping his own bank manager happy. But bear in mind that it's also not an altogether deleterious move to make the *volte-face*. Setting aside the embarrassment of the flip-flop, it shows everyone he's not bound by his purse strings, and with the population numbers moving to the suburbs and to Vancouver Island, the city wants to hold on to brick-and-mortar infrastructure like the port if it doesn't want to end up merely first among equals in the eyes of the province or the feds."

"So, you don't think he was threatened?"

"Sorry, I don't mean to imply that at all. I only mean to say that we are talking about a stratosphere of cynical calculation that is beyond the usual rules of engagement. The great Paul Robeson was once picked up from the airport by a group of young civil rights activists to be taken to an event—Robeson, having gone to Columbia, an Ivy League school, had encountered America's white ruling class in a way almost entirely foreign to the rank-and-file of the movement then, and these young Black men were asking him questions about these rich WASPs the way they might have peppered a space traveller for news about Martians. Apparently, Robeson said to them, 'They're decent people. They love their families. And they will *kill you* over their property.'" The reverend laughed.

"I get the feeling you're a very good priest."

"I'm not bad," she answered, with a wave of her hand. "And I get the feeling that you are a very dedicated psychologist. But I'm worried about you. As well as your patient, and your friend."

"Thank you," said Annick. "I don't know what I'm supposed to be doing right now."

"And yet, here you are," said Carmichael. "Doing it."

19

THE FULL WEIGHT of the day, and of its backdoor neighbour, pressed down on Annick's eyelids like a bully's thumbs as she rode the quiet elevator down into the basement. Her clothes were cold and wet, and her feet were tired, but she knew implicitly that if she stopped to change her clothes, sat for even a second on the bed to strip off the damp socks clinging to her feet like leeches, inertia would pin her inexorably to the spot for the rest of the night, and she needed to see Philip, though she couldn't entirely say why.

On the way out of St. Clare's, Reverend Beatrice had kindly cleared up, to the degree that she could, Annick's initial confusion about the Anglican franchise on St. Clare of Assisi. She then described some of the heavy hitters the British Isles had contributed to the Franciscan tradition across the Middle Ages. There was William of Ockham, he of Occam's Razor, who famously contended that one should always prefer a theory based on the fewest possible assumptions. And from southern Scotland, just outside of what would have been the remit of the medieval Church of England, there was Duns Scotus, a medieval grab bag of philosophical theories, who some people blamed for kicking off modernity.

"For my money, his most interesting idea was *haecceitas*— thisness. Isn't that a beautiful word? *This*ness. Just lovely."

"Sounds very abstract."

"Not at all. It is merely the idea that in a freely created and contingent universe, every creature is made to be precisely the thing that they are."

Annick hadn't sat on the SkyTrain home, for the same reason as she hadn't taken the ride-hail she'd promised Philip she would, and the same reason she hadn't sat to change her socks. As she leaned on the handrail, rocking gently with the train, she turned the idea of thisness over in her mind, set it up against or around the people in her life as a means of making sense of them.

She thought of how entirely alive Danielle had seemed in that YouTube video, playing coyly with the tension between how pretty the audience found her and how jarring they found her sentences; the way she sewed dynamite into nearly musical phrases, gave just exactly the right amount of room to words and ideas.

And there was Ivor—he, too, had his thisness: the hard nose for the story, the carapace under which to set out into what looked, to him, like a crazed world and shout his piece; the soft underside of a widowed husband and bereft father.

She knew Philip's thisness intimately: the scientific mind, interrogative but skeptical, set behind a wry smile that was going to turn up with the slightest, but most loving, condescension at the idea that she had spent the twilight hours of the day at Evensong, with a priest, a mind that understood the world in terms of DNA and RNA rather than haecceitas, but who didn't have to be evangelical about it—who understood that people sought meaning in a matrix of settings, which sometimes seemed designed to deny it of them.

She wouldn't be caught in the mirror this time, knowing that it was there—she stayed pressed to the inside of the short hallway leading into the gym and watched Philip quietly as he worked the heavy bag. Once again, he had the space to himself, but tonight, he wore no headphones. He pounded the bag, throwing a series of straight jabs followed by alternating hooks, and she smiled, and leaned her head against the wall, and actually considered for a moment what it might mean to create a human life with this man she loved. His face was furrowed in exertion, focused with an intensity that made it easy to remember the photos that she'd seen of him as a child; made it easy to imagine what he might have looked like at a small desk at school, tongue jutting out the side of his mouth as a testament to his effort and concentration, his commitment to getting things right. But it also made it easy to imagine his face puckered and wrinkled, his features now just a little too big for their frame, under a head of hair gone white or just gone. And there was the Philip she didn't have to imagine, the one right in front of her—strong, beautiful, hers.

Annick's reverie was broken by a shift in the rhythm of his punching. She stood away from the wall, as Philip stopped alternating his hooks and began hitting the bag with a series of accelerating swings from his right arm, accompanied by an intense and unmeasured grunting. He leaned into the bag, suddenly yelling, nearly screaming, held up standing only by his fists against the leather, and Annick ran to him from across the room.

"Philip!" He was too far gone, at first, to be surprised by her presence, and his first response was to fall into Annick's arms. Then he pushed himself back, confused.

"Where'd you come from?"

"I just came down, *mon coeur*. You weren't in the condo and I knew you'd be down here. *Cher*, what's wrong?"

When his father had died, Philip had not so much cried as allowed the tears to well up in his eyes until they fell. This evening, the same feat of gravity was at work and he dabbed helplessly at his eyes with the cuffs of his boxing gloves. Annick took them off of his hands, which were shaking, and when she took his head to her breast he stopped fighting. She wasn't sure how long they sat that way.

"I couldn't concentrate all day," he said finally, hoarse. "This whole thing—this idea that someone's threatening you, that someone came after you, your friend . . . that all I can do about it is call the cops like some goddamn block-watch captain . . . it's just—it doesn't sit right, you know? It's not how I came up. I mean, I like who I am now, I love our life. But I can't just shake everything else away, you know?"

"*Je sais, mon amour.*"

"I left work at lunch today. And I called Tony."

"Tony? Why Tony?"

Philip sat up out of her embrace and set his jaw. "I wanted—I asked him about maybe putting me back in touch with some people."

"What people, Philip?"

"Some people from the old days."

"Jesus Christ, Philip."

"I just wanted to think it through out loud, with somebody who was there back then with me. To see what my options were."

"Your options for what, Philip? Going to war against the biker gang that runs the city's underworld? Are you out of your tree? I'm standing there in the doorway thinking about us having a baby while you're dreaming up suicide missions with your teenage gangster buddies?"

"I don't like feeling helpless!"

"Holy hell, Philip—do you know anyone who does?"

He shook his head, and they sat in silence for several long moments.

"I'm sorry," he said, and Annick shrugged. "If it makes you feel any better, Tony said basically the same thing. That there's no moving against the Hammer, that it was crazy. They're too big."

"Great. So Anthony Chow is the voice of reason in my relationship."

"There's more. He said the bikers definitely threatened the mayor about the truck route. That's a known thing, apparently, among the people in the loop on the Knight Street stuff. Everybody at Albion Cross. It's an open secret."

"Wait, you told him? Like about the theory and all that? Danielle? Philip how could you do that?! How could you—"

"I *had* to! The story doesn't even make sense otherwise. He's not going to say anything."

"Sure, right, and in this world, if I can't count on Tony's discretion, what can I count on?"

"Bean?"

"Don't *Bean* me, Philip!"

"Annick."

"What?"

"He thinks—Honey, he says it wouldn't surprise him at all if the Hammer killed Danielle. To send a message to Rossi that they were serious. He said it makes sense they'd take out somebody who meant something to him, but that the public wouldn't connect with him in any intimate way. Love, I'm so sorry."

Annick felt a sting at the edges of her eyes, but she was too tired to cry. She nodded her head.

"At least, I don't know," said Philip. "At least you can tell Ivor, and at least you can know, she probably didn't—she didn't take her own life." ·

They stood and weaved towards the door as though both drunk and rode up towards their floor in silence, leaning on each other's shoulders. Each felt a strong claim to first shower rights; both being too tired to argue, they took one long, sexless shower together, alternating turns under the near-scalding stream of purifying water that washed away all memories of the day's rain. Lazily, they grazed on leftovers rather than organizing a dinner, and lay down under the sheets at a bedtime hour typically more appropriate for small children and religious fundamentalists. Annick stared at the ceiling and wondered if a day could possess a thisness.

"Were you really thinking about what it would be like to have a baby with me?" Philip asked, turning to Annick, running his rough hand against the grain of her close-cropped hair.

"No," she said, turning her back towards him and backing her hips and thighs against his front. He slipped an arm around her stomach and she felt herself floating into a soft hypnagogia, just moments away from a sleep too long deferred.

"Tony says Kimberley is starting to show."

"That's nice of him."

"They're talking about names, but he says Kim gets to pick the nickname once the baby's born. It's funny—he was saying how dads don't mind giving kids goofy nicknames, because they didn't have to carry the kid around for nine months, but we'd take it more seriously if we did."

"What?"

Philip laughed softly, nestling his nose and mouth into the nape of her neck. "He said it's hilarious how you guys are born with the eggs in your ovaries, and we don't make the sperm until ten minutes before sex."

Annick pulled away and sat up in bed. "What did you just say?"

20

AS PART OF BECOMING a bona fide West Coaster, Annick had surrendered a certain amount of power over her life to the whims and ways of the BC Ferries corporation. Her dark secret—the admission she couldn't share with Vancouver lifers as they complained about interminable lineups, delayed sailings, reservation fees or nostalgic cafeteria breakfasts no longer extant—was that she loved her trips on these great, shuddering blue and white ships. She couldn't understand how it was that her friends and neighbours could be so oblivious to the privilege of cruising across the Salish Sea— wondering at the craggy, piney beauty of the Inside Passage; letting the salty winds that blew across the wet decks fill your jacket till it felt like you would take off and fly.

The first time she'd flown to Vancouver Island on one of the floatplanes that were constantly taking off and landing outside of her Coal Harbour condo tower, Annick had mourned all of those things—and yet she hadn't been able to shake the mind-breaking feeling that she had somehow escaped the bonds of time. What had been a three- or four hour trip before had collapsed into thirty five minutes spent in an airplane the size of a large van, which was sent humming and hurtling over the water. It was the classic trade-off of long, laborious beauty for efficient, utilitarian performance. She still considered herself, most days, a ferry girl. But today, with the convenience attending to super-villains boarding their private helicopter, she and Philip rode the elevator downstairs and walked the few steps to the float plane terminal.

As Annick approached the ticket counter, she was distracted by the attractiveness of the young man and young woman standing behind the desk, squinting into a shared computer screen with shared frustration. They looked like the young man and young woman who would have been hired to portray the employees of a floatplane airline in a pamphlet or a YouTube commercial. She was small, with delicate hands, and had incandescently black hair pulled into a severe plait; her features were broad and sharp and softened with a generosity of freckles under and around her eyes. He had golden skin almost the same colour as his blond hair and a tiny, debonair moustache that gave him the appearance of an early film star. The expressions on their perfect faces suggested, however, that eternal beauty had been no defence against whichever stumbling block had presented itself before this particular morning. As Philip and Annick laid their hands on the counter, though, the two employees each allowed a phony buoyancy to lift their features, at least briefly, into accommodating service-sector smiles.

"Hi, how can we help you today?" asked the young woman, whose name tag read "Akiko"; her co-worker's said "Wesley."

"Yes, hello," said Annick awkwardly, still tired from the previous night's fitful sleep. "We're hoping to get on the 10:25 to Ganges Harbour? Are there still seats?"

Akiko began to nod slowly, even as a look of solicitous mourning came across her face; Wesley took his cue to return to his squinting at the computer screen. "So, yeah— absolutely there are tickets still available for that flight. I do have to inform you that at present, unfortunately, inclement fog conditions are pushing back our takeoff time, and of course we can't guarantee a hundred percent that the flight will actually be possible at all today."

"Really?"

Akiko nodded sadly, but energetically. "In that event, though, we would have a shuttle a little bit later on that would take you to the ferry terminal and your ticket would be good for bus passage."

"What do you think?" Annick asked Philip. He shrugged with a blank bleakness.

"I mean, it's not like there's a ton of other options, right?" he said. "Besides staying home for a little while, giving this some more thought. We could, I don't know—slow down."

"Is that what you want?"

He looked at her for a moment. "I want to do whatever you think is right."

It was Annick's turn, now, to nod, without any of Akiko's energy. Then she smiled grimly at Philip, albeit with warmth, and turned back to the counter.

"We'll take the tickets, please."

There was a large urn of self-serve coffee on a high table near some large imitation-leather chairs gathered into a waiting area, and Annick filled her paper cup, taking as large a sip as the temperature would allow. The brew was surprisingly hot, and strong, and decent enough as an entry in the category of minor regional airline complimentary self-serve coffee, and she watched a cloud of milk billow to the top of her cup as she wondered if the fog would lift in time for the plane to Salt Spring Island.

"Nice thing about a paper cup," said Philip, "it won't hurt as much when you forget it someplace." She tried to laugh, but her heart wasn't in it. She was in the grip of two contrary desperations: the need to get to Salt Spring as quickly as possible, and the utter certainty that there was no sense whatsoever in going.

They sank into a pair of the false-leather chairs facing in from the windows, and Philip continued to pore over the photos on his phone. Not wanting to distract him, Annick let her attention flit around the rest of the waiting area, surprised by the nearly unanimous stoicism which seemed to hold sway over the passengers who might or might not be flying out that morning; might or might not be passengers at all. Standing out amidst the gallery of quiet, fatalistic resignation was a woman in her late fifties or early sixties, cooing warmly and elaborately into the tablet in her hands, through which Annick could only surmise she was communicating with a baby grandchild.

Annick watched the woman play and replay a short pantomime circuit of larger-than-life but recognizable human emotions and responses across her face. She had evidently stumbled upon the seemingly random string of sounds or expressions that drew trills of laughter from a now-giddy infant, and would continue to do so for as long as she was willing to keep going. The miserliness of adult laughter, coming only once for a joke if the teller was lucky, seemed especially stingy and austere compared to the infinite fount of children's laughter, which couldn't be stopped once it started except with effort, and lost none of its lustre with the retelling of a gag. Kids didn't have to be surprised in order for something to be funny—why was that? Annick supposed that everything was still so new, the world still so lacking in context, that everything seemed an absurd incongruity alongside absolutely everything else.

Of course, from the baby's point of view, the grandmother, too, was experiencing a joy every bit as unsusceptible to decrease by repetition.

"Nope, it's . . ." Philip said, fading off into a vague frustration, with himself or the situation. "I can't figure it out from the pictures."

"It's okay, *cher*—we'll figure it out. People on the island must know the place."

Philip continued as though he hadn't heard her. "I'd know the place to see it, for sure. He sent a shot from the driveway the first day they got there. And they're on the water, obviously, but I can't tell what they're looking out at."

"Stupid question, but if you search 'Miles Truscott, Salt Spring Island home,' anything?"

"Nothing."

"Of course not." She tried to sip from her now-empty cup. Lowering it back down to her knee, she looked again at the face of the grandmother, still smiling, but now clearly speaking to an adult at the other end of the call. As she watched, the quality of the light on the woman's face began to change, brightening, and Annick turned in her seat to look out the window, where outside the fog was thinning and the rain was slowing to a spit.

"Hey," she said, tapping Philip on the shoulder. "That's looking pretty good. Maybe we'll be flying out this morning after all."

"Fat lot of good it'll do us if we don't know where the house is."

Annick slumped back down in her seat, tapping the empty cup against her knee before standing back up and walking to the coffee urn, pouring herself another cup. She took this one black. She looked at the faces of the beautiful employees behind the counter and tried to divine from their countenances whether she'd been right about the turn in the weather. If there was good news on the way, they were hiding it well. She walked back over to her seat and sat down.

"Did you try googling that pretentious name he had for the place?" she asked. "The one Tony told us at Mykonos?"

"Ah, Toronto something? Toronto . . . super . . ."

"God you're lucky you're pretty, boy. No, it was Italian. *Tramonto. Tramonto . . . Sopra Vesuvio.*"

"That's a pretty good pull."

"Hey, when Philomena Conte is your mentor, you develop a bit of an ear. But it stuck with me more because I just remember thinking it was so obnoxious that he would give his Gulf Island residence an Italian name."

"I think once you're in naming-your-manor territory, all bets are off. What does it mean?"

"You're the one who grew up in East Van."

"What do you want from me? I'm uncultured, okay? I eat the food and the rest isn't my business."

"*Tramonto* is 'sunshine' or 'sunlight' or something having to do with the sun, I think? Dr. Conte would kill me. Hold on." She tapped into her phone. "Sun*set*. So *Tramonto Sopra Vesuvio* means 'Sunset over Vesuvius.'"

"Okay. A poetic if slightly awkward construction, I guess."

"But why an Italian name? I still don't get it."

"Wait, Vesuvius—why does that sound familiar?"

"Jeez, you're really going for full bimbo points today, huh? It's the volcano, in Italy."

"No, not that," said Philip with put-on contempt for the idea that he could be that dense, as he opened a map of Salt Spring Island on his phone. "Here," he said, smiling now, and pointing at the northwestern corner of the island. "Vesuvius. Vesuvius Bay Road. And this road, running up from it . . ."

"Sunset," she said, smiling.

"Ladies and gentleman, thank you for flying Harbourfront Airlines this morning. All passengers destined for Ganges Harbour on Salt Spring Island, please have your boarding passes ready and prepare to board at the gate."

21

THE WETNESS OF THE ISLAND was lush and verdant, transforming entirely the effect of drops that fell in the same way here that they did on the mainland, seeping into every surface—but redounding, here, in a fecund riot of vitality. Instead of the mildew rippling across the ceilings of poorly ventilated city basement suites, here the life beckoned by the rain emerged as massive evergreens, somehow cradling more than looming, their boughs heavy with water that would make its way down to a ground cover of ferns and salal which shattered the colour green into a greater number of hues and shades than Annick had even known existed. The rain made sense here, she thought. To see it in this context—falling not on concrete or patio umbrellas but into root systems, which had come up through millions of years of evolution just to drink it. Not soaking shirt collars or children's socks but long, bright, elegant leaves, which held the moisture in jeweller's beads all along a pendulous flirtation with the forest floor—you couldn't be mad at it.

The pearly sky was holding overheard, but already losing some of its light with the oncoming creep of the afternoon. The flight over had been the shortest period Annick had ever been on a plane, but also an entirely different sensory experience from any other airborne trip. The constant sound of the propellers had been intrusive enough to make conversation with Philip, in the seat next to her, nearly impossible. The plane was so much smaller than what she was used to, and flew so much lower to the surface, that it had felt almost like an entirely novel mode of transport. The earth wasn't far enough beneath them to become a grid of abstractions, some cloud-covered map of the world below. She could see waves and farms, the details of houses; every swell of wind or passing air pocket shook her, too; made itself entirely felt. It was a somehow more primordial version of flight—immeasurably closer, she imagined, to the trips taken by the early aviators than were the flying cruise ships delivering passengers from Los Angeles to Amsterdam.

When they had landed at Ganges Harbour, the car they rented was ladybug red; Annick had suggested a stop at the liquor store for a bottle of wine to soften their unexpected arrival, though Philip hadn't thought the subterfuge would get them very far. Now they made their way painfully slowly up Sunset, north of Vesuvius, hoping for signs of the waterfront mansion of which Tony had sent Philip so many tantalizing photos.

"This is hopeless. What are we supposed to do?" said Annick from the passenger seat, craning for a better view through the furious pounding of the windshield wipers. "Are we just going to drive up every driveway on the street?"

Philip shrugged. "It backs onto the water, so we know it's on the left. I think the thing that makes the most sense, I mean—yeah? Drive up as far north as the road will take us, then turn around so it's on our right. And start peeking up driveways."

"*Merde.*"

They travelled in silence up Sunset Drive. On Annick's side, there were properties of varying sizes—some modest; some large, rolling farms.

"Look," she said, tapping Philip lightly on the hand, and he turned to see a family of deer—a doe, buck and fawn grazing roadside with an air of somehow panicked nonchalance, and Annick smiled and lowered her window as they passed, in order to get a better view. "*Petite famille d'amour.*"

"Jesus, what time is it?" said Philip, breaking the spell. "Deer are crepuscular. If they're already out we're losing light."

"Deer are *what*? God I love it when you talk science to me."

Philip affected a casual smile, but rolled his eyes theatrically. "*Cre-pus-cu-lar,*" he said, drawing the syllables out. "They only move around at dawn and dusk."

"See, to me, you know what you have there?"

"What's that?" he bit, sighing.

"You have a word that needs to be explained every time it gets used. Which I'm afraid makes it a failed word. It just didn't catch on, you know? Which is a problem, because that's all a word is supposed to do—mean something to people. Like your crazy one the other time, for the music in the movie, it's coming from in the scene—"

"Diegetic."

"That's the one. How many times do you think someone can say 'diegetic' without immediately having to say, afterwards, 'that means music the characters in the movie can hear'? Honest guess? One in three thou—"

Philip jammed his foot violently into the brake, sending the car into a squealing fishtail up the middle of the street for ten yards. When they stopped, the sound of the rain hammering the roof was deafening.

"What happened? Was it another deer?"

Philip smiled wildly at Annick, then reached over and pinched the side of her belly, raising his eyebrows. She slapped his hand.

"What the hell is wrong with you?"

He smiled and pulled the small red car into an easy U-turn, retracing about thirty feet of the road. He pulled into a perfectly smooth asphalt driveway, next to a tasteful cedar wood sign with gold cursive lettering:

Tramonto Sopra Vesuvio

"You sweet crepuscular son of a bitch."

⁂

Since arriving on the island, Annick had noted a great number of buildings done in West Coast fancy-dress cabin style, a mode of McMansion in the guise of rustic chalet that she associated with the ski resorts at Whistler, and whose architectural, not to say cultural, sensibility had radiated out across Canada's Pacific Coast to wherever any amount of money had pooled. These buildings strained for a kind of backwoods humility with heated floors, suggestive of warm hearths built around roaring fires on dimmer switches. But Tramonto Sopra Vesuvio was done in the East Coast style of the sturdy, impassive, cedar-shingled monuments to inter-generational New England fortunes that dotted the more idyllic deposits of countryside around Halifax. Driving past those summer residences on family day trips as a youth, Annick—who had squinted from the back seat—experienced each miniature Kennedy compound with feelings of intimi-dation and resentment that passed as a kind of dull wonder. When they weren't Americans, the people inside these kinds of houses had, by dint of their being the sorts of people with beautiful summer homes, a real stake in the country, its institutions, the way in which it was run. These types of places were where the people exhausted from determining the fates of the nation came to drink shandies and put up their feet.

Against the already-darkening afternoon sky, the house was lit from within like a jack-o'-lantern and they stood for a second at the doors of the rental car, taking it in, as the rain fell in fat drops on their faces.

"Tony's car." Philip said by way of confirmation. Annick raised the bottle of wine in an ironic show of confidence, took a deep breath and closed her door.

A large, beautiful copper bell hung to the right of the door, with a dark, tobacco-coloured leather strap hanging from its clapper. On this particular bell though, which was the size of an opened parasol, the combination of form and function was not intuitive.

"Are we supposed to ring that?" Annick asked.

"I doubt it."

"Why else would there be a bell there?"

"It's just rich people shit, man," Philip said, leaning forward and knocking on the door. His knuckles resonated feebly against it, and for several seconds there was no response. He knocked again, and they waited.

"I don't think anybody can hear you. The place is huge. I'm sure we're supposed to ring the bell."

"The guy's a real estate tycoon, he's not going to have some hillbilly doorbell for letting cowboys know when the chili's ready."

"Cowboys?! Look at that thing. It belongs at the back of an orchestra pit."

"So ring it if you're so sure."

Annick shifted the wine bottle to her left hand and took the leather handle tentatively with her right. She rigidly jerked the bell's uvula against its side and produced only a flat clang along with a sarcastic snicker from Philip. Shooting him a look and mouthing a silent curse in his direction, she limbered her wrist, striking the bell in a supple, voluptuous motion that produced a clear, sonorous resonance.

"There." She said with terse pride and a stiff, satisfied nod. "Now I feel like I should be praying."

"I've been praying since that plane took off," said Philip, facing the door.

There was finally motion behind the thin strips of stained-glass window that framed the doorway, and now Tony, in a T-shirt tight against his enormous arms, chest and shoulders, opened the door, standing his body in the space he created.

"Phil. What are you doing here, man?"

"Surprise! We were on the island bro; we wanted to surprise you."

"You should have called, man."

"Called to tell you we were surprising you?"

"How did you get here?"

"We came over on the floatplane. We've got a hotel for the night, last minute. Couldn't take the city in the rain anymore. Bro, you gonna let us in? It's soaking out here."

"You should have called. How did you find the place?"

"We were gonna try to ask somebody," Annick interjected with an overly cheerful enthusiasm. "But Philip actually figured it out from the name! Sunset Over Vesuvio."

"What do you mean?"

"*Tramonto* means 'sunset,'" Philip said, taking a different tack, allowing a measure of flintiness to come into his voice for the first time. "Dude what's up, why are you acting weird? You don't want us to come in or what?"

"What? I'm not acting weird, no. Sorry, I'm just—no, I'm surprised, that's all. You just caught me off guard. It's good to see you guys."

Philip pressed the advantage, jocularly shooting a feinting punch at Tony's mid-section, causing him to flinch. "What do you need to be on guard for, hey? You're on island time, man! Now show me this mansion you've been teasing me with, bro. I want to see if it lives up to the pictures."

Tony smiled weakly. "Sure. Yeah, come in."

"We brought wine," Annick added, hoisting the bottle.

Tony took it from her hand with a nod, without its having been offered, and held the bottle from its neck as though he were casually trailing a club.

The immaculate walls of the Truscott island home were mounted with track-lit original artworks, running from traditional and contemporary Indigenous carvings and prints to the well-lit staged photography of the Vancouver School. Annick realized that in all her years of passing by these sorts of houses, it had never occurred to her to imagine their interiors. Even now, with money of her own, she lacked the imaginative insight for furnishing the homes of Those Who Never Had to Worry Again. In the homes of regular people, everything looked comfortable, and inviting, because it had been worn threadbare; in the homes of those with a bit of money, things were harshly beautiful but sterile, touched sparingly or with great care because they couldn't be easily replaced. But in the houses of the rich, things could be beautiful and they could be welcoming, because the very best objects had been obtained by those who felt not only that they deserved them, but also that they could replace them if they had to. Couches that would be treated like nuclear submarines by other families had fleece blankets folded over their backs; dining room tables which held space like concert pianos actually had plates of food left on them. The Truscott home *smelled* rich; had that ineffable scent which promised that nothing bad had ever been cooked or eaten within these walls; no one unwholesomely tired or dirty had ever been inside.

As they came into the large, open sitting room, facing a wall of windows that looked out onto the waters that separated the island from the Cowichan Valley, Annick gasped quite sincerely at the beauty of the scene. She turned and waved at Kimberley, who stood in a thick men's flannel housecoat, smiling with polite surprise next to a cream-coloured chair, looking just a little bit more pregnant than the last time they had seen her.

"Hey!" she exclaimed.

"Pop-in! Sorry-slash-surprise-slash-hello!"

"Wow," Philip said with an air of masculine obsequious-ness, looking out onto the view. "That's unreal."

"Crazy, huh?" said Tony. Annick watched his grip on the wine bottle out of the corner of her eye. "Babe, they're at a hotel on the island tonight, just stopped by to surprise us. They figured out where the house was from the name."

"How?"

"You guys ever see killer whales?" Philip asked. "Orcas?"

Kimberley nodded. "Once, yeah. We saw three."

"Too cool."

"Can I pour that wine?" Annick asked.

"So where are you guys staying?" asked Tony.

"Some hotel," said Philip. "I don't even remember the name. Nice, though."

"Don't remember the name? Little weird."

"Dude, I'm so fried. Why do you think we needed the vacation?"

"Yeah?"

"Yeah, things at work have been—it's just been really rough."

"Well, good that you were able to get out in the middle of the week, then."

Philip nodded.

"Tony," Annick said, "this is so rude, because we brought it, but I am just dying for a glass of that wine."

Tony surveyed the room. "Sure. I'll go pour. Kimmy, you keep everybody entertained in here."

Annick smiled and wandered the periphery of the living room, gravitating towards the large, round stone fireplace that acted as a hinge between it and the dining area. She held her damp arms out towards the softly crackling fire inside, and she noticed that the elegant four-piece wrought-iron hearth set which sat next to the grate was missing its poker.

"I'm so sorry, Kimberley, we completely blanked on bringing something you could drink," Annick said, turning from the fire.

"Oh, that's okay. Miles keeps this place super stocked. There's a massive pantry and another fridge downstairs, plus a coffin freezer."

"Yeah?" said Philip.

Kimberley nodded. "We never need to go out for anything, seriously. And there's always tons of juice, sparkling water, whatever. I'm all good."

Annick smiled tightly. Philip nodded good-naturedly.

"Yeah," said Kimberley.

Tony came back in with the bottle in hand and a glass of the wine, and gave the latter to Annick.

"Thank you so much," she said. "You're not having any?"

Tony shook his head. "No, it's not fair to preggo over there." Kimberley rolled her eyes.

"Okay, well—I guess I'm drinking alone then," said Annick, and lifted her glass in a small almost-toast before taking a long sip. "Oh, that's really nice."

"You bought it," said Tony.

"Guilty as charged," said Annick.

"Come on, let's have a seat," said Tony, sweeping his arms in an ushering motion after setting the bottle down on a side table.

"Actually, could I use the washroom first?" asked Annick.

"Sure, it's right behind you," Tony said, pointing to a powder room in the hallway just off the living room. Annick stared down into the depths of her wineglass.

"This is, um, incredibly embarrassing, but . . . is there one I could use that might have . . . oh my God . . . like, a little more privacy?" Annick drew a sharp intake of breath through an ingratiating grimace, and the upward inflection of her sentence had nearly lifted her off the floor.

Tony waved his hand dismissively. "Dude, it's fine."

"Tony, come on," Philip said with cajoling reason. "You know how it is, man, you're on the road . . ."

Tony gave a small sigh. "Okay, Kimmy'll take you to one of the other bathrooms."

"I'm sure I can find it."

"No it's okay, Kimmy will show you."

Annick nodded and smiled. She set down her wineglass on a cork coaster next to a tall, black table lamp and followed Kimberley out of the room.

"Have fun," said Philip from behind her.

"Ew, gross," she replied.

The two women smiled awkwardly at each other in the hallway, following the corridor back down to the foyer where they'd entered the house, and off a hallway leading to a den and a split staircase.

"This place is amazing," Annick said with innocent excitement once they were out of easy range of the living room. "I'm dying to see the rest of it."

"Yeah, I don't know if—" Kimberley began, when Annick made a confident turn for the stairs and took the first steps down without asking. "Oh, I don't think we should—"

"Is there a bathroom down here?" Annick asked broadly, loudly, turning on lights as she moved down the hallway of the downstairs floor.

"Annick, we're not supposed to be here," said Kimberley, her voice poking at the edges of politeness, trying to assert herself without indicating that anything was wrong. "Annick?"

"What do you mean?" Annick was guileless in her words, all furtive hunter in the movement of her eyes, her head and hands. Her fingers sought out switches with a manic energy as she scanned every space she could with the jerky panic of a woman who wasn't certain where she was looking, or what for. "Truscott doesn't let you guys use this part of the house?"

"No, it's not that." She was making up the distance between them with faster steps now. "Annick, stop."

She did. She spun on her heels and took Kimberley by the shoulders, pushing her into an open bedroom behind her and closing the door.

"What the fuck, Annick?"

"Kimberley, is Danielle still alive, or isn't she?"

"I—what?"

Annick shook her head. "You know what I'm talking about. Is she alive? Is she still here?" Kimberley's eyes widened and her mouth opened to scream for Tony. Annick quickly clamped a hand over Kimberley's mouth and saw the current of fear coursing through the pregnant woman. Annick tried to speak with a gentleness inversely proportionate to the firm grip with which she held the bottom half of Kimberley's face.

"Kimberley, you're feeling all kinds of anxious sensations right now, but I need you to know that you are not in any danger, okay? Just breathe in through your nose. Long, deep breaths. Your heart is racing, that's perfectly normal. You are perfectly safe. Your baby is perfectly safe. I'm a psychologist. You know that, right?" Kimberley nodded hysterically. Tears streamed down her cheeks. "It's okay. You're okay. I'm covering your mouth because I can't let you warn Tony, not yet. But I'm a psychologist, Kimberley, and that means I know people—and I know what kind of person you are. I know you're not a kidnapper and I know you're not a murderer." Kimberley whimpered. "Kimberley? You're a good person. I know you're a good person. I need your help, okay? Kimberley? Is Danielle here?"

Kimberley nodded.

"Is she alive?"

Kimberley closed her eyes. When she opened them, tears were now running in rivulets down her face.

She nodded.

Annick lurched forward onto the bed, her hand still firmly covering Kimberley's mouth. For a moment Annick didn't realize what had happened, wondering if there was someone else in the room, if she had been sapped from behind. It was several moments before she realized that her knees had simply buckled.

She sat the both of them up on the bed and smiled as warmly as she could at Kimberley, locking her eyes with a pair now nearly as shining wet.

"Kimberley, I can't imagine the depth of feeling that must connect you to the little life that is beginning inside of you. Only I know a man who feels something like it for Danielle. He brought her into the world, same as you're bringing that baby into it. And the only thing he wants is to have her back. I feel like you must be able to put yourself, however little bit, in those shoes. To want to know that your baby is okay. That the life you gave them is intact. Honey, just tell me where she is, give me enough of a head start to get to her and then you scream for Tony, okay? Will you do that for me?"

A dam of tears built up at the front of Kimberley's eyes, then broke silently on her eyelashes, pouring down her cheeks, her perfectly still face, to Annick's hand. She nodded slowly.

"Sweetie, I'm going to take my hand off your mouth now. I'm putting all the trust I have in the world in you."

She nodded again. Annick winced as she removed her palm from over Kimberley's mouth.

"I tried to tell him to call the police, as soon as we got here. But Miles was so mad that he brought me; I was scared. Tony didn't know this is what we were coming for, he—" she gave a sobbing laugh, "he thought he was getting a promotion. Miles always held that part of Tony—" Kimberley seemed to startle suddenly, choked from her own words, as though she were waking from sleep apnea. "I can't have my baby in jail, Annick. We can't both go to prison. We can't. Annick, you're hurting me."

Annick hadn't realized that she had begun digging her nails into Kimberley's shoulders—not deliberately, but through a sheer attempt at containing the rage and pity vying for control of her response. *If you didn't want to have your baby in prison,* she wanted to scream, *maybe you shouldn't have helped to kidnap someone else's. Maybe you should've indicated a spine, rather than played the pure passive accessory to the kidnap of my patient.* From another angle, though, Kimberley really was a hapless accomplice, if that was the word; maybe even a kind of second-order victim. And wasn't she showing that spine now? She could have screamed for Tony.

"Kimberley, listen to me. When Danielle is free, Philip and I will tell the police, the lawyers, whomever—we will tell them that you phoned us."

"What?"

"We will tell them that *you* are the reason we knew to come here, okay? Just tell me where Danielle is, right now. And if you ever show a moral failure like this again in your life, so help me Christ I will throw you to the fucking killer whales myself."

"At the end of this hallway," Kimberley said in a hoarse, shaky whisper, "there's a billiards room. Off that, there's a big bathroom with a sauna at the end of it. She's in there. It's not on or anything," she said, following the look of concern on Annick's face. "That's just where she is. Annick? Thank you."

Annick squeezed Kimberley's shoulders once more. "Thank *you*." She stood from the bed and ran down the hall.

She couldn't remember the sequence that spilled her through the billiards room, past the large snooker table and into a granite-tiled bathroom as big as a community centre changeroom. Her focus returned as she saw the thick cedar door of a sauna, a wrought-iron fireplace poker run through its door handle as a makeshift lock. She wrenched the poker from the doorway and threw the entrance open, and she and Danielle came together like a pair of cymbals at an aria's crescendo.

That's when Kimberley screamed for Tony.

Tony was down the stairs with an animal speed, and he knew without having to be told that his problems were in the billiards room. As he filled the doorway on the other side of the wide expanse of smooth, green felt on the table in front of them, Annick could read the wild fluctuations in his facial features, the pulsing alternations between fight and flight, predator and prey. For all his speed he hadn't yet decided, consciously or unconsciously, whether he'd caught her or she'd caught him, whether he was feeling furious or exposed, fit to plead or to start barking orders. The only certain thing was the churning instability of his energy, jagged and deadly.

"Listen. No one was going to hurt her, just—it was Miles, so if we all . . . listen, fuck, you just put her right back in— get the fuck, both of you . . ." Tony's speech was mercurial and uncanny, his whole aspect uncoupled from some vital, human anchor.

"Okay Tony," Annick said with soft assertion. "But Danielle is leaving now, with us, and we're—"

"No." Tony spoke softly, looking at the floor, the ceiling. His head shook and twitched with the jerky power of dead-end thoughts and short-circuiting strategies.

"Yes," said Annick.

"I said *no!*" he shouted, lunging forward.

Annick shielded Danielle with wild swings of the fire-place poker, and Tony began picking bright red snooker balls from the rack next to him and pitching them with a ferocious power in their direction, leaving enormous holes in the wall behind the two women with every throw. Then a sheet of purple cascaded down his face and it was seconds before Annick realized that Philip had brought the wine bottle crashing down on the top of his skull.

Lurching wildly, Tony spun, grabbing successfully for a cue but bringing the wall-rack down thunderously in the process, sending eight-ball and snooker balls across the floor. He swung the cue like a baseball bat, making a perfect connection with Philip's left shoulder, but Philip screamed into a vicious series of right hooks to Tony's ribs.

Annick tried desperately for a chance at Tony with the poker, but the two men were in too tightly for her to risk it. The men's bestial grunting was shrilled through with Kimberley's screaming from the doorway, and now Tony slipped the cue behind Philip's back, levering him up slightly from the floor with it. Knowing that Philip's left arm was out of commission, Tony angled the cue against his right shoulder, moving it down towards the elbow, trying to make it an even pair. When Tony readjusted the stick momentarily for better purchase, Philip thrust his forehead into Tony's nose, breaking it. As the larger man rolled off him, instinctively cradling his face, Philip grabbed the bright blue two-ball from where it had fallen on the floor, hitting Tony until he was unconscious.

Annick ran out of the room, taking the stairs three at a time, ripping her phone from her jacket pocket in the front hall. Jamming 9-1-1 into her phone, she heard nothing; looking down, she saw she had no service. Letting out a half-sob, half-scream, she exploded from the front door. She took the bell-clapper in her hand, and rang it as hard and as long as she could, calling as loudly as possible for whoever might come.

22

NO ONE HAD SAID SO explicitly, but Annick assumed that the front door to Tramonto Sopra Vesuvio was being left open for Danielle's sake. There were no huge teams of police officers parading in and out over the threshold—not yet, anyway, though there probably would be a decent contingent once Mountie reinforcements and higher-ups were sent in from the mainland and Vancouver Island.

For the time being, there were just two constables from the Salt Spring detachment of the RCMP, who had begun to move through the house after taking initial statements, and two paramedics who had run some preliminary checks on Danielle, Philip and Tony. Another Mountie had escorted Kimberley to the police building on Lower Ganges Road for questioning, while two more officers had left with Tony for the Madrona Bay heliport, where they would meet the RCMP helicopter as it arrived from Comox; from there he would be flown to the helipad at Vancouver General Hospital, just a few blocks from City Hall. Danielle and Philip, and with them Annick, would also be taken to the VGH helipad, but in an air ambulance they were told might still be a while given the rains and the relatively non-acute nature of their injuries.

For now, they sat under blankets in the foyer, the cold, wet November air inrushing Miles Truscott's immaculate home. The door had been propped open, which seemed like a promise to Danielle, a reassurance that she was no longer shut in the house. Even still, every few minutes Danielle would shudder and start, half shooting forward from where she was sitting, and grab hold of Annick as if to keep from falling. Now she would cry, now stop. Philip did his best to telegraph distance with his facial expressions, to project the idea that Danielle was safely with Annick, that he wouldn't pry. Annick held her patient in her arms like a mother, without clinical detachment. There had been no specific instructions from Dr. Conte about a situation like this.

"Alberto and I, during the campaign? We used to meet sometimes on Miles's boat. This British yacht he moors at Granville Island, like something out of the movies. I'm such a fucking idiot—it was so romantic, though."

"You are the furthest thing from an idiot, Danielle."

"Miles told me Berto wanted to see me on the boat. He wanted to see me, but—there was no reason it should have been him telling me, that's the thing I keep kicking myself for. Miles had never been the one to set anything like that up, the go-between. And I even knew him and Alberto had been arguing about Knight Street. But . . ." She smiled ruefully, shaking her head. "Alberto had just dumped me. He was trying to get me to go to LA or Toronto, said he knew some producers—he was just throwing me away, you know? It hurt so much, I thought he I wanted to think we were meeting because he changed his mind."

"Oh, sweetie," Annick said, accepting Danielle's sobs into her shoulder. "You didn't do anything wrong. Do you understand me? I am not going to let you blame yourself for this. *You didn't do anything wrong.*"

"I didn't even know what was happening. On the boat Miles said we were going to meet Berto over here. That Miles's wife was coming and we were going to have a whole couples' weekend. *Stupid.* It was just so surreal. I didn't even realize I'd been kidnapped — he didn't even take my phone. By the time you get to his place, there's no service."

"Yeah, I figured that one out myself," said Annick.

Danielle sat back up on the bench and readjusted the blanket around her shoulders, shaking her head in disbelief. Annick watched her face as it shifted like a weather system, beneath eyes staring into the half-distance. For a split second, the way it sometimes would during even in their darkest sessions, the pain and terror cleared to make space for the mischievous, ironic Danielle, a persona who Dr. Boudreau had learned could never be entirely banished, no matter how bleak the situation.

"Who do you think will play me in the movie?" she asked.

"Gilbert Gottfried," Annick said, and rubbed the side of Danielle's arm as her patient leaned up against her and laughed.

"Is this it for me though?" Danielle asked, still smiling but now unmistakably serious.

"What? Why do you say that?"

"I was already so fucked up. Now this," she said, indicating the house around them. "How am I ever supposed to come back from this?"

"You are selling yourself far, far too short, *mon amie*. I want you to think of where you were at just a few months ago. How far you've come."

"A few months ago I was ready to kill myself," Danielle said, nodding. "I even kept the note, like, I don't know—some perverted kind of insurance policy. I couldn't throw it away. And what gets me out of my funk? I fall in love with some married asshole who won't call the cops when I've been taken hostage because he still hopes that things can end quietly."

"That's not true, Danielle. I was there, I saw you at those lowest times. I'll tell you right now, you could never have had a relationship at the place you used to be in. However it ended up, whoever these guys ended up showing you they really were, that campaign brought out your smarts and your talents, and it drew people to you because you're magnificent and you're meant for it. None of that's got anything to do with anyone else being bottom feeders or snakes or any other of the million and one kinds of scumbag you're going to come across in the world. You're a gift, Danielle. To the rest of us but just as much to yourself. This is one of the worst things to ever happen to one of my patients—and I don't for a second doubt you'll come back from this."

Danielle stared straight-ahead for a few moments, then turned to Dr. Boudreau with a sad smile. She leaned her head on Annick's shoulder, and closed her eyes.

M

There was no precedent for a municipal by-election called two weeks after the general election itself, and even waiting until the new year began felt somehow premature. The City had turned in wide-eyed terror to the Province and to the Feds, and an array of constitutional, political and other legal scholars had been drafted into service in order to determine the proper way forward. But for the time being, Olivia Preston was acting mayor of Vancouver, as police coyly dangled the possibility of criminal consequences for Alberto Rossi, beyond the far-reaching and irreversible political and marital ones that had already been meted out to him.

Tony Chow hadn't been willing to go down without Miles Truscott, and Miles Truscott—a load-bearing wall— wasn't going down without taking everyone else with him, including the friend and candidate whom he had nurtured meticulously and bankrolled since nearly the beginning.

But Chow had fairly roared the full tale from a pit of resentment that had opened up inside him and swallowed all three men. The reformed tough guy routine had not been a ruse for Tony; his work at Albion had been a genuine attempt to channel his youthful brio and violence and predation into the channels of acceptable masculine sociopathy and the matrix of the real estate market, but Truscott, the prep school thoroughbred, had refused to let him change— had sniffed out the goon that he needed and pressed him to work. Now Tony wouldn't ever get to run to the pharmacy in the middle of the night for his baby, read stories or sing songs or learn to rock and sway mid-conversation as a matter of second nature like the other fathers did.

So wounded, Tony had shouted the story loudly enough that anyone could hear it: how in his first week as the new mayor, Alberto Rossi had been approached by two full-patch members of Satan's Hammer, albeit wearing suits and accompanied by a lawyer. The lawyer's intervention had been engineered not so much to highlight the strength of the Hammer members' non-existent legal case, but more to outline their extensive knowledge of the Rossi family's comings and goings; in tortured legal prose, the lawyer's memo had obliquely alluded to the mayor's wife's place of business, his children's schools and even the assisted-living apartments where his parents and in-laws lived. According to Chow, Rossi had folded immediately in the face of the threats, reversing his Knight Street truck route policy nearly on the spot.

But this was a decision that had failed spectacularly to take into account the commercial interests of his patron and companion, Miles Truscott. Albion had stood, conservatively, to make tens of millions of dollars from the sudden upzoning of the land assemblies they had amassed all along the length of the soon-to-be-former trucking route along the full length of the city's east side. Truscott had been apoplectic, but the way Chow had it figured, Rossi was not only terrified of the bikers but saw the possible silver lining of the decision in the chance to permanently reverse the power dynamic between him and his piggy bank, now that he was mayor.

And so Truscott had lashed out with the only threat he had left: he would go public with the fact that Rossi was having an affair with a young member of his campaign staff. But

Rossi knew that Truscott would be slow to immolate the political asset he'd spent all these years cultivating, and that there was no paper or electronic evidence of his affair; he had also been confronted by one of his lieutenants who had given him an ultimatum, demanding that he end the romance with Danielle. When Truscott had realized that Rossi was ending things with her—might even in fact be thinking of facilitating a move for her, a soft landing in Toronto or LA or some other town capable of keeping a comedy writer at least partly employed—that's when, in a panic, he moved on Danielle.

Over the years, Rossi and Truscott had been city journalists' favourite unlikely duo: the gregarious, left-leaning, labour movement–bred politician and the quiet, plotting, old money éminence grise; the Dreamer and the Realist. But it was Rossi who, over the course of Danielle's kidnapping, had emerged the cold-blooded negotiator. It had quickly become clear, even to Danielle, that while Truscott may have prevented Rossi from sending her quietly off someplace where the news of their relationship could be kept safely submerged, he had accomplished little else. Once it was obvious that Rossi wouldn't compromise himself by rushing to the island, the negotiations had shifted to an emphasis on threats against Danielle herself. When even this new tack produced no change in Rossi's position, it was she who had realized that the mayor was perfectly willing to let Truscott eliminate the only evidence of his single most compromising indiscretion. It was a moment of incandescently sombre epiphany which had simultaneously broken her heart and, likely, saved her life: Danielle had pointed out to Tony that if anything happened to her, the only clear winner was the mayor, and for a few days that had seemed to work. But it had begun to dawn on her, through Tony's growing brusqueness, punctuated by moments of solicitous near-kindness, that Truscott had figured out the extent of his miscalculation, and was inevitably going to draw the operation down. In order to guarantee Tony's silence, Danielle reckoned that he would be the one tasked with disposing of her. And all that she could think about, upon that realization, was that she had worked so hard to convince herself to live—and now someone else was going to take it all away.

✱

When the air ambulance had landed on the VGH helipad, Ivor—wearing every bit of his beating and his stay just a few floors down across the surface of skin bruised to multicolour and stitched closed above and beside the temples—was waiting. Tears were welling in his purpled eyes when Danielle came off the plane, as tears were streaming down her otherwise impassive face, still bearing the markers of shell-shock. Split seconds of disoriented hesitation echoing out from the trauma of her ordeal and the memories of their estrangement shot through her gait as she nevertheless fairly ran into her father's arms. They held each other there for several minutes. Neither the writer nor the comedian could find any words equal to the needs of the moment.

Danielle turned back to Dr. Boudreau, wiping her eyes with the back of her hand, then her nose with the back of her sleeve. Her face was now a humid red mess of tears. "Do I look okay?"

Annick laughed. "I'm going to leave you with your dad now, is that okay?"

"Totally."

"We need to get Philip downstairs, make sure his arm and shoulder are going to be okay."

"Of course. Can you please let us know?"

"Absolutely."

Several more tears rolled down Danielle's large, beautiful face, though she didn't seem to notice them. "It is literally impossible for me to ever thank you enough, Dr. Boudreau. I don't even know what to say."

Annick smiled and squeezed Danielle's arm. "Seeing you here is going to carry me through to summer, Danielle," she said, her voice very nearly breaking. "I was so worried about you."

"I could never kill myself, Dr. Boudreau," Danielle said. "I have way too many browser tabs open."

However badly she'd needed the joke, Annick wasn't ready for it, and the laughter almost hurt.

"I'm around over Christmas, okay? And you have my number. We'll take all the time we need to on this."

"Okay. Thanks, Dr. Boudreau," she answered, still snuffling and wiping at her nose.

"Annick?" Ivor's bottom lip was trembling, and he shook his head at her dumbfounded. As the long seconds wore on, his speechlessness intensified, taking on almost comic proportions, his palms turned helplessly upward, tears running down his cheeks, and Annick gently took his battered body into her arms.

"Thank you," he said.

"You're welcome," she answered, staying in the hug through several tightening squeezes that spoke a sort of grateful Morse code. She kissed Ivor's cheeks and stepped back. "I'm going to go take care of Philip now."

Danielle leaned in. "We don't ever have to talk about this again, like, in a clinical setting? But—he is so fucking hot."

Dr. Boudreau nodded.

✳

"Check the internet."

"I think she's right, I think that's how the tradition got started. Like what would go bad?"

"It's a food product."

"Yeah, but with no moisture. That's how popcorn pops: the water in the kernel heats and explodes."

"Who's the science journalist now?"

"Oh, I'll remember that remark next time you venture an amateur psychological appraisal, Dr. Lee."

"*One* year! It says 'popcorn garlands should be disposed of at the end of each Christmas season'—Mom, take it down, that's disgusting! How many years have you been putting that same one up?"

Denise Lee dismissed her son with a contemptuous wave of her hand, without looking away from the tree in the corner of her living room. "They just try to get you to buy more popcorn."

"Yeah, that's right Mom. We're just lining Orville Redenbacher's pockets."

"Look at that," said Annick, pointing out through the window of the living room into the nighttime street. It's snowing again." Still looking out the window with a crooked smile, Philip extended his hand towards her, twinkling his fingers; she took it in hers. Without words, they slipped on shoes, and went out onto the front doorstep, leaving Denise to dress her tree with heirloom foodstuffs.

The city glowed a warm and brilliant white against the weight of the early evening midnight, and Philip slipped his arm around Annick's waist as countless soft, fat snowflakes fell soundlessly on the equally quiet neighbourhood.

"You think it'll last for Christmas?"

Philip shrugged. "It never does."

"Not even three days?"

"Snow doesn't belong in the city. It lives in the mountains."

She wrapped both her arms around his middle. "It's nice."

"Yeah."

They stood silently in the moment for as long as it lasted, felt the wrestle between the chill of the winter air and the warmth of their embrace, and wondered at the uncanny silence of snow-cushioned nights. Philip leaned and kissed Annick on the top of her head.

"You want an eggnog?"

"Oh, that's revolting. You think I'm going to drink an egg-nog without rum?"

"I mean, you could probably have a little rum. We don't know if anything's happened yet."

Annick smiled and shook her head, and held her love closer.

THE END

Author's Notes & Acknowledgements

THIS STORY WAS CONCEIVED, set and mostly written in the city I love—which happens also to be a city built on the unceded, ancestral territories of the Musqueam, Squamish and Tsleil-Waututh Nations. Vancouver has made up a tiny fraction of the history of these lands, and I hope that our town's future will involve our being more humble, respectful and accommodating neighbours than we have been. We might find some clues for a better way of living together in the history of Vancouver's very first labour union—which was, in fact, a waterfront union. The so-called Bows & Arrows local of the Industrial Workers of the World, the city's first union local, was made up largely of Indigenous waterfront labourers. As BC author Tom Hawthorn has written, in 1920 Vancouver longshoremen fielded an integrated baseball team that included players who were European, Black, Squamish and Indigenous Hawaiian. The labour movement, in general and on the waterfront specifically, has been an overwhelming force for good in this city, and a few bad apples, in a mystery novel storyline or the odd newspaper report, should do nothing to distract from that.

Because this story involves so many fictionalized Vancouver institutions and elements it feels even more incumbent upon me than usual to stress that it is entirely fictional, and that aside from Dr. Boudreau and a couple of restaurant staff no one in the story is even particularly inspired by or remotely intended to be a composite of any actual persons. That said, Chris Higgins did offer early, much-appreciated insight into what it would involve if the city did want to draw down the truck route. Any and all public and political figures who appear in this book are entirely fictitious, and I mean that; I'm not trying to be cute. I did work as the election campaign joke-writer for BC NDP leaders Adrian Dix and John Horgan (as well as briefly, for the latter, while he was premier), but I must assure you, not without a little regret, that there was zero intrigue involved in either case. I borrowed one of the jokes Adrian actually did tell at the Vancouver Board of Trade ("Theoretical Marxism Thursdays") for Danielle's portfolio.

Reverend Beatrice's story about Paul Robeson is lifted from my late friend Jack O'Dell, one of the unsung heroes of the twentieth-century Civil Rights and labour movements, who was one of the young men in the car with Robeson when he said what he did. Beatrice's Franciscan knowledge was provided by the writings of Mary Beth Ingham, Ilia Delio, William Short and Richard Rohr.

Thank you to Toby Hargrave and my mother-in-law, Pauline Tong, from whom I pilfered the bitter melon episode. Only Toby never learned to love it. Thanks also to my mother-in-law for help with the Cantonese dialogue.

Mariwan Jaaf is the progenitor of the term "Fat Man Parking." *Spas*, bro.

Andreas Schroeder and Sharon Brown provided me with the use of their legendary writers' cabin and, as always, I am struck speechless by their grace and generosity.

These acknowledgements are being typed on a computer that Donovan Deschner not only loaned me but drove to my hotel when I forgot to bring my computer with me to Calgary to finish edits—you're a mensch!

Thank you to Carrie Taylor, Auntie Sue and Auntie Connie, Annie Martin, John Munro, Iona Whishaw, F. at Chronicles of Crime and everyone else who reached out with kind and encouraging words about the first Dr. Boudreau book, *Primary Obsessions*—including my brother, Nick, to whom I dedicate this book. Thank you also to his partner, Chris, for answering any floatplane-related questions. It meant so much to me. Anu Sahota Henderson's observations about the sameness of Vancouver café design (offered in conversation at Victoria's very-not-Vancouver-caféish Murchie's tea room) were the inspiration for the imagined interior of Bean Through the City. Thanks to Sam Wiebe, Paul Finch and Rob Simmons for your friendship and support, and to Ashleigh Ball, my fellow Beat Bug, for letting me use her lyrics as my epigraph.

Thank you to my publisher Anna Comfort O'Keeffe for your pandemic patience (which is endemic) and everyone at Douglas & McIntyre in Canada and Legend Times in the UK. Enormous thanks to my editor, Caroline Skelton, for making it possible to do this. Thanks as well to my agents John Pearce and Chris Casuccio at Westwood Creative. Sincere appreciation also to ZG Stories for all your hard work publicizing the book.

Also, no one would be reading this without booksellers, librarians or teachers—thank you all.

Thank you to my real-life "Dr. Boudreau," who has seen me at the darkest pits of depression more times than

I could count. Someone recently brought to my attention a quote from the late author Mark Fisher, who was, tragically, overwhelmed by his own struggle with depression. Fisher wrote, "[T]he depressive is always confident of one thing: that he is without illusions." There were times, during the pandemic-era writing of this book, in which I was beset by utterly stupefying and paralyzing bouts of depression. I can't think of a more important insight than Fisher's to hold onto in that moment: you are not seeing things more clearly. Depression is the distortion. With help, we'll get through it.

Love to my dad and Dwight, to all my aunts and uncles and cousins (and their little ones); *grosses bises à Mamie*, Alberte Boudreau; and to my daughter, Joséphine, and wife, Cara, around whom I can never stay in the dark long about the real meaning of life.

CHARLES DEMERS is an author, comedian, voice actor and playwright. He is one of the most frequently returning stars of CBC Radio's smash-hit comedy *The Debaters*, with a weekly listening audience of 750,000. His collection of essays, *Vancouver Special* (Arsenal Pulp Press, 2009), was shortlisted for the Hubert Evans Non-Fiction Prize. He is also the author of *The Horrors* (Douglas & McIntyre, 2015), *Property Values* (Arsenal Pulp Press, 2018) and *Primary Obsessions* (Douglas & McIntyre, 2020). The latter is Demers' first book in the Doctor Annick Boudreau Mystery Series, for which he draws upon his own long-time experience with cognitive behavioural therapy. Demers lives with his wife and daughter in Vancouver, BC.